"Moira comes first," he said softly

"In everything I do. I want you to understand that, Molly. I need a great deal of money so that if I can't buy her a cure, I can buy her a comfortable life."

"I understand, Tim." Almost unconsciously, her head tilted sideways and landed on his broad shoulder.

"So for the next few months, I'm going to play shark in the money sea. It'll take me all hours of the day and night, and I expect it'll throw me in with some strange bedfellows. But I'm going to do it."

"Strange bedfellows" struck Molly as a vulnerable point. "You mustn't go so far that Moira won't recognize who you are," she returned.

"You object?" His voice was suddenly cold, harsh.

"I don't have the right to object, Tim," she said firmly.

Emma Goldrick describes herself as a grandmother first and an author second. She was born and raised in Puerto Rico where she met her husband, a career military man from Massachusetts. His postings took them all over the world, which often led to mishaps—such as the Christmas they arrived in Germany before their furniture. Emma uses the places she's been as backgrounds for her books, but just in case she runs short of settings, this prolific author and her husband are always making new travel plans.

Books by Emma Goldrick

HARLEQUIN ROMANCE
2661—THE ROAD
2739—THE TROUBLE WITH BRIDGES
2846—TEMPERED BY FIRE
2858—KING OF THE HILL
2889—TEMPORARY PARAGON
2943—TO TAME A TYCOON
2967—THE LATIMORE BRIDE
2984—PILGRIM'S PROMISE

HARLEQUIN PRESENTS
841—RENT-A-BRIDE LTD.
866—DAUGHTER OF THE SEA
890—THE OVER-MOUNTAIN MAN
953—HIDDEN TREASURES
1035—IF LOVE BE BLIND
1087—MY BROTHER'S KEEPER
1208—MADELEINE'S MARRIAGE
1281—A HEART AS BIG AS TEXAS

Don't miss any of our special offers. Write to us at the following address for information on our newest releases.

Harlequin Reader Service
P.O. Box 1397, Buffalo, NY 14240
Canadian address: P.O. Box 603,
Fort Erie, Ont. L2A 5X3

THE GIRL HE LEFT BEHIND

Emma Goldrick

Harlequin Books

TORONTO • NEW YORK • LONDON
AMSTERDAM • PARIS • SYDNEY • HAMBURG
STOCKHOLM • ATHENS • TOKYO • MILAN

Original hardcover edition published in 1990
by Mills & Boon Limited

ISBN 0-373-03111-4

Harlequin Romance first edition March 1991

To Margaret and Jim,
in the hope that they might forgive us
for moving the village boundaries
five hundred yards farther west.

THE GIRL HE LEFT BEHIND

CHAPTER ONE

MOLLY PATTERSON came around the curve in the road in her old Nissan and looked happily at her own house, poised on the cliffs above the grey Atlantic Ocean. Although she had been born and raised in the old Steamboat Gothic mansion overlooking Kettle Cove on Cape Ann, it still tugged at her heart whenever she had been away for a time. There was a strange car parked in front of the steps, and a man was sitting comfortably on the top stair, waiting.

She blinked her eyes nervously, trying vainly to focus on him, as she took her glasses off. Excessive pride dictated that she not wear the gold-rimmed spectacles, even if she was somewhat near-sighted. In months past she would have blundered along and made any visitor welcome. But since she had won the Lottery some six weeks earlier, Molly Patterson had grown up quickly. Not the megabucks millions, of course, just the weekly pay-off. Enough money so she could afford to take a year's sabbatical from her teaching job. And just in time, too, in the light of the considerable mess she had made about Alfred! Seventy thousand dollars, minus the taxes. And the tax men took their bite out of the cheque before Molly had even seen it. Nevertheless, in a small community, sixty thousand was a substantial attraction. And she had been too stupid to realise that Alfred could count that high without using his fingers and toes!

'Molly?' The figure on the stairs stood up, seeming to stretch endlessly. There was something about the face, gaunt and tired and unshaven. Something about the untidy mass of brown hair, bleached by the sun in places, fluttering in the offshore breeze. Something about the dark blue eyes. Something about the tall thin frame, thin almost to emaciation, but loaded with cable-muscles, as well she knew!

She fumbled for the first step as her mind flashed back. Pictures crowded in on her, imposing themselves one on top of another, each not quite obliterating the scene in front of her.

Six-year-old Molly; he was eight. 'It won't hurt, Molly, honest. And we have to do it because we're friends, aren't we?'

'But I'm scared, Tim! The knife is sharp, and——'

'And then we put our fingers together and we're sealed in blood, Molly, and we'll be loyal friends forever!' But it did hurt, and she cried, and nothing could soothe her spirit until her mother covered it with two Band-aids. And then she could boast, because not many of her friends had a finger with a bandage that size. As for Tim, you couldn't put a bandage on the place where *he* hurt after his father found out about it!

Twelve-year-old Molly; he was fourteen, sitting at the foot of the apple tree where he had fallen, holding his broken arm with the other hand. She had screamed her head off and run, while he kept back the tears. He had worn a cast for six weeks that summer, just because she had demanded that he rescue her cat—who didn't need rescuing. The animal had spit and scratched at Tim until his hand slipped and he fell. And when Molly's mother heard all the details she had marched her daughter off to her room and—but that was not the sort of thing worth thinking about!

Thirteen-year-old Molly; he was fifteen. They were at

the bottom of the sea-cliff. The cold rock towered above them, with hardly a foothold to be seen.

'It's easy,' he coaxed. 'Just follow me. Put your hands where I put mine, and don't look down.' Blindly trusting, she had done so, until halfway up the sixty-foot cliff she'd lost her nerve and clung sobbing to the tiny ledge which provided just enough space for her toes to gain a hold.

'Come on,' he had teased gently, but she had not had the heart. He had cajoled for ten minutes, and then left her to her tears. She had thought the world was surely done with her, but then he was back with ropes and tackle, talking gently to her from the top of the cliff as he set his anchors. And he was beside her.

'Hold tight to me, Molly.' Of course she did. Despite all her fears she clung to him as he gradually brought them up the face of the cliff to safety.

'I shouldn't have done that,' said the suddenly mature Tim. 'I shouldn't have dared you to climb like that.' But all Molly could think of was that she had trusted him with her life, and he had not failed her.

Eighteen-year-old Molly; he was twenty, with his parents divorced and gone away. And that was the year that her cousin Susan came to spend the summer. A summer of sheer misery, because eighteen-year-old Molly was a woman grown, but tall, gawky and all bones, while nineteen-year-old Susan was petite, blonde, all curves and smiles. And that summer Molly found out that she was the fifth wheel on the cart, and it ended dismally when Susan said, 'And of course you'll be my bridesmaid, Molly.' Molly's mother had smiled sweetly and her father beamed, and there was hardly any time for Molly to say, 'No, I'd rather cut your heart out!'

With an artificial smile on her face she had gone to the bottom step with the rest of the wedding party, and had thrown confetti, wishing it were bombs. Susan had aimed her bouquet, and it landed in Molly's hand. So long ago. Every female at the wedding had either died of old age or was married, Molly reminded herself grimly. Even the flower-girl. Everybody except Molly Patterson!

So Susan took Tim away, and the house next door grew empty and started to fall down, and Molly had lost both her parents to the sea and won the lottery, and now she was twenty-eight, with an old dog, and a heart that ached only occasionally, and settled in her little niche in life, and ——

'Tim?' Her voice was dry, raspy, fighting the emotion that stormed at her heart. Or rather a combination of emotions—love, hate, memory, anguish. Her body froze on that bottom stair. He came rumbling down and his arms were around her and it was warm, and the years peeled off like a patch being removed. She ducked her head into the heavy flannel shirt he was wearing, and closed her eyes. It almost seemed as if once again she was the girl next door—but then one can never go back, can one?

Molly sighed, broke away from him, and knuckled at the little tear that formed in her eye. It had been ten years since her last hug from Tim, and the cracked heart she thought had been repaired turned out to have been papered over rather than cemented.

But I'm not going to go through all that, she told herself fiercely. You had your share of Molly Patterson, Tim. And I'm not going to let you have another bite!

He crushed her close again, his face buried in her long straw-coloured hair. 'God, what a fool I've been, Molly!' he groaned in her ear. Silently, cool-headed, dependable Molly agreed with him.

* * *

'Tell me about it,' she prompted, as she brought the hot coffee over to the big kitchen table. Enough time had elapsed for her to control the wild beating of her heart, to salve the reopened wounds. Enough time so that she could act as a nonchalant friend. She had always been a good actress, going back to the shared days at Gloucester High School. But then so had he. Come on now, she told herself firmly, don't make a big thing out of this. He belongs to Susan!

Tim warmed his hands on the coffee-mug. November on the high sea cliffs north of Boston was always a chilly time. 'I don't know how to begin,' he sighed. 'I need help—so where else would I look but to Molly Patterson?' He stared into the black of his steaming coffee, then sipped, all without looking at her.

She slid into the chair across from him, feeling more than a little anger. 'After ten years, Tim? With never a word?' He had the grace to blush. Almost she could see the boy in the face of the man. Almost.

'Yeah, I'm probably as welcome as the tax-collector.' His deep voice was no longer smooth and suave. There were cracks in it, as there were on his forehead. And there was a trace of embarrassment. The Tim she had known could never have hesitated about asking for help—especially from Molly Patterson!

'That's not true.' She forced a chuckle, wondering if he could hear how false it was. 'You're always welcome here. Remember, we sealed a bond for life?' She grinned as she held up her thumb. 'And I've still got the scar to prove it!'

He reached across the table and took her wrist. A hard, callused hand, thin but muscled, with fingers that could outreach hers by half. He turned her palm over and traced the scar. 'God, there's no end to the trouble I've caused, is there?' he muttered.

Molly mustered up her best smile. 'Come on now, Tim, if we were to add up the scars and bruises we've each inflicted on the other it would come out even. So life has its drawbacks. Lay your problem on me. That's what friends are for.'

That managed to bring a little smile, a little upward quirk at the corners of his mouth, a tiny gleam in his sea-blue eyes.

'Nothing's hurt you. You haven't changed a bit. I'm glad for you, Moll.'

No, nothing's hurt me—lately—she thought to herself. How could anything else hurt me after your wedding, Tim? She ducked her head to hide the bitterness.

'Well, among other things it's the money,' he said flatly. Her head popped up and she stared at him.

'The money? The sole heir to the Holland millions? What are you doing, Tim? Teasing me?'

'Not a single tease,' he sighed. 'The money's practically all gone. It never amounted to millions anyway. There might have been *one* million, but if my father had spent twenty dollars we would have fallen out of the class. Then, when my mother split, she took him for considerably more than half of it. And Susan and I, we led each other a mad, mad chase. In Europe, mostly. She loved Paris, I did too, for a time. But, you know, the night life got to be pretty boring. I had a lot of acquaintances, Molly, but no friends. Susan had a lot of—friends.'

'Drink your coffee,' she nagged him, and got up to top up his mug. 'So all the money's gone?'

'Not all,' he told her. 'There's still the fishing fleet and the freezer plant, and a few pieces of real estate, and some other things here and there, but it's slipping out of my hands. I need to be able to settle in one place and concentrate on Holland Ocean Fisheries, Incorporated. If I work hard enough at it I'm sure I can re-establish things, and get over the hump.' He slammed his fist down on the table. Both coffee-mugs jumped, and Molly's spilled over. She gave a vague swipe at it with a paper napkin.

'But I—I don't understand,' she said softly. The situation was getting out of control. Where, but a moment ago, she had anticipated giving him a hard set-down, now all of a sudden she was unable to mask her interest. 'Of course I'll do anything I can to help, but what about Susan? Where is she?'

'I haven't the slightest idea,' he snapped, and she could see his fingernails biting into the palms of his hands. 'When I told her the money tap was shut off, so was she. I haven't seen Susan for well over seven years.'

'But I still don't understand, Tim. What do you want from me? Money?'

He pushed his chair back, rasping it across the old linoleum. 'Money?' he asked sarcastically as he struggled to his feet. 'God, I'm tired! We drove all the way up from Washington today. No, I don't need money from you, Molly. I thought you of all people would understand!'

She jumped to her feet too, anger lighting her green eyes. 'Well, I would if you'd only stop feeling sorry for yourself, Tim Holland, and explain to me exactly what's going on! Now you just sit down and shut up! I mean—start talking!'

He grinned at her, and for a moment the daredevil Tim was back. Across the table from her he rubbed a hand across the stubble on his face. 'Among other things, what I need, Molly, is a little straightforward honesty.'

'So sit,' she said. You'll get all the straightforward honesty you can stand, she thought grimly. And then some. He grinned again and dropped back into the chair. 'And now,' she said, following suit, 'you can start off by telling me just who the "we" are that drove all the way up here from Washington! If Susan's not with you, who is?'

Tim held his hands out in mock supplication. 'I keep forgetting you don't know all that much about me lately,' he grimaced. 'There's Moira to consider.'

Molly shook her head, trying to clear the cobwebs, and asked the obvious question.

'Moira's my daughter,' Tim told her apologetically.

'Well, where in the world is she?' She glared at him, and the sudden movement sent her long silky red-gold hair swinging across her face. She pushed it out of the way and re-tied the old pink ribbon that held everything in a ponytail.

'She's asleep,' he said. 'Out in the car. She talked all the way up to Boston, then she sort of keeled over and fell asleep. Moira's my problem, Molly. I need someone to look after her while I put my heart and soul into this rescue mission. A matter of two or three months, no more.'

Molly was not the dunce of the Patterson family. The whole story was revealed in three sentences, and despite her resolve, she accepted the burden. 'Well, you'd darn well better bring her in,' she ordered peremptorily. 'Imagine the nerve of the man, leaving a little girl out there all by herself!' She wanted desperately to be angry with him, but one look at that crooked smile, the head slightly cocked to one side, was more than her sobriety could stand. After all, he *was* Tim, and she was the girl next door. A tiny smile sneaked out from under her anger.

'Ah, that's my Molly,' said Tim as he got to his feet and headed for the door.

No, that's *not* your Molly, she thought as she watched

his broad back disappear through the door. He slammed it behind him, of course. Hadn't he always? I'm *not* your Molly. Dear God, I always wanted to *be* your Molly, but I didn't make it, did I, Tim? Always cast as the best friend, but never the lover. If I had any sense, Tim Holland, I'd print me a sign that says 'Molly Loves Tim is Past History,' and I'd put a tenpenny spike through it, and take up my hammer and nail it right on to your forehead so the words were forever in front of your eyes—your *damn* eyes!

The clatter of feet snapped her out of her reverie, as the door opened and Tim came in, his daughter close behind him. His daughter! A tiny little thing with an elfin face and long straight blonde hair, a pointed chin and a big smile that came to an abrupt halt when the child saw Molly. The little girl stepped behind her father, one hand clutching his coat sleeve, effectively hiding as her father made the introductions.

Molly was fastened to her chair. The little girl was all Susan. Every inch of her was her mother—except—no, the little girl had brown eyes, rather than the startlingly violet orbs that Susan was so vain about. Molly shook herself mentally, then stood up gracefully and smiled. 'Welcome to my home, Moira,' she said softly.

The child remained in hiding behind the huge bulk of her father, her face poised between sun and rain. Luckily Shag came wandering in at just that moment. A brown and white St Bernard, grey-muzzled with age, a hundred and fifty pounds of creaking overweight pure-bred, Shag owned Molly, the house, and the acre of scrubland around it, and he knew it. He wandered vaguely across the floor, favouring his arthritic hindquarter, and sat down directly in front of the little girl.

'Ooh,' said Moira, 'he's big for a dog!' The child's

voice had that flat quality, that lack of stable tone that Molly recognised immediately. And then the girl looked Molly up and down and added, 'So are you.'

'Moira!' Tim was still holding his daughter's hand. He gave it a shake and looked just a little displeased. The child peered up at him.

'I mean, the dog looks big for a dog and she looks big for a girl, Daddy.' With which she moved around behind him again, like a child trying to hide from a lightning blast.

'*Molly*,' her father insisted. 'Her name isn't *she*, it's Molly. And the dog's name is Shag.'

'You know the dog?' The little girl peered out from behind him, her curiosity overcoming her nervousness.

He ruffled her hair with a gentle hand. 'Of course I do,' he chuckled. 'He was just a pup. I gave him to Molly on her fourteenth birthday.'

'Fifteen,' Molly interjected in the interest of accuracy. It had been a lovely gift; the finest she was to receive for many a year. And now she and her dog were years older and decades out of touch.

'Yes,' Tim continued, 'Molly spent a week agonising over what to call him. Seems to me I remember a great many tears——'

'Well, girls of fifteen tend to be emotional,' she snapped at him as she blinked back another tear. Too many memories, all crowding in on her. They *must* be stuffed back in the storage bag! Cool, calm Molly Patterson. Pragmatic. Phlegmatic. She sniffed a couple of times.

'So at the end of the week, when she was still shilly-shallying,' Tim continued, 'I named the animal for her—Shaggy Dog. Which then gradually became Shag. Hey, old mutt?'

Shag lifted his huge head as if it were a burden, and his tail wagged, once to the right, once to the left, and then down on the floor with a massive thump. His jaw fell open, displaying an array of massive teeth, and the dark rough tongue licked at the extended hand.

'He remembers,' Tim said softly, looking over the child's bright head at Molly. She nodded slowly.

'Could I ——?' The little girl looked up at Molly, the question big in her eyes.

'Of course,' said Molly. 'Put both your hands out very slowly. Don't touch him—just put your hands in front of him so he can smell.'

The child complied. The old dog cocked his head, sniffed for a second, and licked. Moira squeaked, her hands shaking, but did not pull back.

'Say his name, then scratch his ears,' Molly instructed.

'Shag? Shag?' The exquisitely formed little hands moved slowly, and the treat began. The huge drooping ears fluttered. Shag leaned forward to get the fingers in just the right place, and made a happy noise.

After a moment the child looked up at Molly again. 'Shag,' she said firmly. 'But what do I call you? It's not polite to call adults by their first name—my dad taught me that.'

'That's all right,' Molly soothed. 'I can be *she* if that's what you want. Or Molly, if you like that better. Or—well, I *am* your mother's cousin, Moira. That makes me a sort of aunt. Would that be better? Aunt Molly?'

The child bit at the bait, came out from her father's shadow, and moved over to the table. She talked to Molly, but her eyes were all on Shag, who sat making vague scratching motions with his hind paw, and missing what he was trying to reach, the corner behind his straggly left ear.

'Aunt Molly? You knew my mother?' There was an anxious look in her little face. 'Was she pretty?'

'The most beautiful girl in Magnolia,' Molly said solemnly.

'Magnolia? Where's that?'

'That's here,' said Molly. 'This whole place is a village called Magnolia. Are you hungry?'

'When is she not?' Tim interjected with a grin. 'She looks like a stick, but eats like a horse!'

'Daddy!' One little foot stamped imperiously on the floor as Moira glared up at him.

'Oh, excuse me,' he chuckled. 'I forgot that we're grown up now.'

'He can't help it,' the little girl apologised in a strangely adult way. 'He's only a man, you know.'

'Yes, I know.' Molly grinned down at the solemn little face. 'I've known your dad since he was a little boy, and he never did know how to deal with girls! Now, what would you like to eat?'

It was no surprise to discover that the child wanted a hamburger. Molly prepared the only patty she had unfrozen, and made an omelette for Tim and herself. And as she worked she wondered. Strange, that a child could seem so young, and yet act in so mature a manner! There was a mystery here, for sure.

'I don't keep much out of the freezer,' she explained as they gathered around the table. 'And I don't heat the house often, either, only the kitchen and the bathroom. But since Moira's going to stay a while, I'll get everything going.'

'Does that mean you're accepting the challenge?' he asked. She stared at the tentative look on his face. Not handsome, she remembered, but nice. And worried.

'Of course it does,' she returned. 'It's a very convenient

time. I don't happen to be teaching this semester, and have a lot of time on my hands. Why? Was there ever any doubt? What are friends for?'

He shook his head, smiling, acknowledging the debt with his eyes as he scanned the kitchen. 'Not home much?' He gave her a look that bespoke a thousand questions, which Molly had no intention of answering. 'Hey, I'm sorry.'

'No need to apologise,' she laughed. 'No, I'm not home much. Up until two weeks ago I was working as a Special Needs teacher for the Essex School District.'

'No longer?' He leaned both elbows on the table and stared at her. The single overhead pull-down light, right over the centre of the table, cast his face into planes and shadows, making him unreadable.

'No,' she sighed as she pushed back her chair and started to clear the table. 'No longer.' And I'm darned if I'm going to tell you about *that* fiasco, she thought. 'I had a thought that I might go back to get another degree, but—well, I've become a terrible procrastinator, Tim.'

'I doubt that, Molly.' He pulled back his chair and came to help. She waved him off.

'Moira and I can take care of this little bit.' Molly looked over at the little girl, who was still busy with the sponge cake dessert. The child was facing away from them and seemed totally oblivious to their conversation. Another clue fell into place as Molly considered. Throughout the last two hours, every time Tim wanted to speak to the child he had moved directly in front of her!

'Then I'll leave you two to it.' Tim broke into her thoughts, wiping his hands off on the apron she wore over her slacks. 'I've got to hustle down to Boston and find a place to rest my head.'

'What the devil are you talking about?' Molly slapped

gently at the masculine hand that was toying with her hair. 'And don't think you can get away with teasing me to change the subject. Times have changed.'

'So they have,' he laughed. 'But it's true. I have to find some little den close to the action, and——'

'*You* haven't changed a bit, Tim Holland,' she grumbled at him. 'Still the same arrogant, insensitive boy I've always known! I have a lot of bedrooms in this house, all unoccupied. I'm twenty-eight years old, for goodness' sake, and a spinster to boot. You're not going to damage my reputation by moving in with me for a few months, and you're *not* going to get away with just dumping your daughter on me while you run for the bright lights of the city. You'll make your headquarters right here; I've got plenty of room, you can be with your daughter, there's a telephone, and Highway 128 is hardly ten minutes from our door. And that's the way it's going to be!'

Moira had turned around to look at them, her face as bright as springtime. 'There, she told you off, Daddy. 'Bout time too!'

'She certainly did, poppet.' He plucked the little girl out of her chair and hugged her before whirling her around in a circle over his head. She screamed in excitement, and was laughing deliriously as he gently lowered her to her feet.

'Aren't you going to whirl Molly?' The child looked at both of them expectantly. Molly put up both hands in self-defence and backed away.

'I don't think she wants to play,' sighed Tim. 'And that being the case, suppose I drive back to Gloucester and pick up all our gear. I dropped it off at the Cape Ann Motor Inn, figuring that might have to be our home for a while. It won't take long. You'll be all right, Moira?'

The child was all solemnity again as she smoothed

down her little dress and looked at the floor. 'I think so,' she said. 'Only you have to promise to come right back. I like your friend—Aunt Molly—but——'

Aunt Molly backed up against the solid support of the kitchen sink and watched as the pair of them made communion. He knelt down in front of the child and offered both hands. The girl took them, then squealed in laughter and received a kiss on her cheek as her father winked at her and stood up. There seemed to be no place for a third party in this closed community; Molly felt a little lump in her throat and turned away to hide the tiny droplet that seemed intent on escaping from her left eye. *She could have been my daughter*!

Tim started for the door. His little daughter coughed conspicuously and tapped her foot. He caught himself in mid-stride, turned and came back to where Molly was standing. 'Thank you again for everything, Moll,' he said. 'A fellow doesn't realise who his friends are until he really gets in a bind.' As he had with his daughter, he reached out both hands to take and squeeze hers, and kissed her gently on her forehead.

Molly didn't dare to answer. How could she possibly yell at the man, with his daughter watching? How could she possibly tell him that a kiss on the forehead would just *not* do? How could she tell him that she didn't want to be his *old friend* any more? Instead of words she tendered a tiny smile, and finally started breathing again when she heard the motor in his car start up.

'Now then, Miss Moira Holland,' she said. 'How about you?'

'How about me what?' The little girl went rigid and stood her ground.

'Well, for one thing,' Molly smiled, 'who's been buying your dresses lately? That one you're wearing is short enough to— give you a considerable chill this winter. Are all your dresses the same?'

Moira looked down at the little gingham thing that clung to her bodice and ended three inches above her knees. 'My dad buys all my clothes,' she said. Again that solemnity that rules when a child has lived most of her life with adults instead of other children. But then her head shook, her little tongue protruded for a moment. 'He don't know much about girl clothes. That's why I wear a lot of jeans. He thinks I like them.'

'And how come he thinks you like them?'

''Cause I tell him so. It's the only way I can keep my bottom warm!'

Now don't start off trying to reform some other person's children, Molly told herself sternly. Mind your own business! But if he's placing the child in *my* care I think we'll go down on Lexington Avenue and have a shopping afternoon. And then there's school, and we need more groceries, and I'd better see about milk delivery, and I need to have the oil tank filled for the furnace, and—good lord, I thought I'd spend the winter in splendid isolation!

The bathroom was a comfortable seventy degrees when she managed to coax Moira upstairs some time later. The little girl was a silent shadow, doubts registering on her face at every step. Without her clothing she was a chunky little thing, big for her age, splashing gently away in the huge old-fashioned tub, at times relaxed enough to show the child through the adult veneer.

As Molly carefully contained the long blonde hair in a plastic shower-cap, the little girl fumbled with her right ear and put something on the chair beside the tub. Conversation seemed to cease after that. She would make a statement or ask a question, then duck under the water and come up in a spray of water. Molly rolled up her sleeves and scrubbed Moira's back. The game went on until the water in the tub began to cool.

'You'd better climb out now,' Molly said quietly. She was kneeling down by the tub at Moira's side. The child stilled instantly, and turned to stare at her.

And that's the final clue, Molly told herself grimly. Slowly, without actually making a sound, she mouthed the same words. Moira nodded, and scrambled to her feet. She's reading my lips, Molly sighed to herself. Not yet eight, and she's reading my lips! She struggled to mask her emotions as she pulled a big bath towel from the rack and wrapped the little girl within it.

The first thing that Moira did when her feet hit the rug outside the tub was to rub her right ear with the towel, and reach over to re-insert the little hearing aid. 'That's nice,' she said. 'I love splashing baths. Mrs Morriset, she didn't like splashing.'

'I don't mind a little splash,' Molly responded. 'I was champion splasher in this house at one time. Did you know that?'

'Really truly?'

'Really truly. And do you know something else? My mother told me that your dad and I often had baths together in this very tub—of course we were little then.' And how about *that* for a way to get to a child's heart, Molly chided herself. She absolutely adores her father. What a lucky man!

Molly talked on as her hands scrubbed at the child with the towel. 'You have a lovely name—Moira. I like that. It's an old Irish name, you know.'

'Is it?' With her head barely visible among the folds of the towel, the little girl finally managed a grin. 'Do you know what it means?'

'Well, yes and no,' Molly chuckled as she pulled one of her old linen shirts over the child's head to serve as a nightgown. 'Actually it's the same name as mine, deep down. It's the same as Mame, Molly, Polly—oh, there are a dozen nicknames that go with it. But essentially it means Mary. And that's from the Hebrew—and that's all I'm going to tell you tonight. Come on now, hop into bed.'

The corridor outside the bathroom was cooler. They ran the length of it, holding hands, and Moira vaulted into the canopied bed and was under the covers before Molly could catch her breath. Moira sat up, with the quilt pulled up to her chin.

'Aunt Molly,' she said, squirming, but never taking her eyes from Molly's face, 'you haven't said a word.'

'About what, dear?'

'About my hearing aid. Mrs Morriset said it made me look ugly.'

Molly's anger, always on a quick fuse anyway, almost burst through the top of her head. 'She lied, my dear,' she said forcefully. 'You're beautiful. Who was this woman?'

'She was our—housekeeper, I guess. She was one of those friends of Daddy's. Why would you want to know?'

Because I'm related to Lizzie Borden, Molly wanted to shout, but didn't. And I'd like to get out my little axe and give that fool woman forty whacks—or more, for that matter! 'Oh, I was just curious,' she said. 'I suppose your dad had a lot of woman friends?'

'There were plenty,' sighed Moira. 'Daddy didn't seem to keep girlfriends long. Some day we oughta talk to him about that, don't you think? You being such an old friend of his and all?'

'Well, perhaps we might,' Molly responded carefully. 'Your dad is a fine man. He's big and strong and intelligent and——'

'Good-looking,' his daughter prompted drowsily, just before she fell off to sleep.

'Yes, and good-looking,' Molly whispered softly. 'And dumb, dumb, dumb, dumb! Damn the man!'

She heard the noise as his car drove up outside. Not quite wanting to leave the little girl alone on her first night in a strange bed and house, she backed out to the open door of the hallway and waited.

Tim joined her in a moment, bringing with him the chill of the November night. His cheeks were red, he was puffing from the exertion, but the devil gleamed in his eye.

'If she's asleep now, she'll sleep till morning,' he whispered. Molly nodded and led him to the room next door, the one he had always used when he stayed over, those long years before. Ten minutes later he joined her downstairs.

'There are drinks in the cabinet.' She waved towards the old mahogany sideboard that had been her father's favourite piece of furniture. 'There's not much of a choice, but you're welcome.'

He walked across the room, inspected, and made his choice. 'You're not having any?'

'No,' she said, sitting down primly on the edge of the couch. 'I—don't drink alcohol any more. And I wanted to ask you a question.'

'Only one? You're a paragon, Molly!'

'Only one,' she sighed. 'Tell me about her hearing.'

Tim sank back in the overstuffed chair opposite her, took a sip that half emptied his glass, then considered.

'I suppose you think that's none of my business, asking a question like that?' she asked warily.

'No, not at all,' he returned. 'It's something Moira and

I have come to accept—and Susan would not. And you need to know if we're going to spend the winter together.

'Good God!' Molly cried. 'Susan abandoned her because she's hard of hearing?'

'Not entirely,' he answered bitterly. 'By the time Moira was six months old the doctors had determined that she suffered from a degenerative congenital hearing loss. She can't hear at all in her left ear; her right ear is gradually losing its response. The doctors say that by the time she reaches puberty she'll be totally deaf.' His shoulders seemed to sag at the end of the statement. 'And that *and* the money were too much for Susan. She bugged out one night—cleaned out her closet and my bank account, and that's the last we've seen of her.'

'Hearing problems are a hard thing to face,' Molly said quietly. 'I've been doing a great deal of work with special interest children at school. Moira has years ahead of her; she can learn all the other communications means. She can already read lips, and I can teach her sign language. And by the time she's twelve, who knows what the world of medicine might have learned to cure!'

'You don't understand, Molly.' Tim stood up, gulped down the remainder of his drink, and set the glass down hard on the end table by his chair.

'Don't give me that *you don't understand* business,' she snapped as she stood up to face him. Her height was her advantage. Although he was over six feet, she was five foot eleven herself, in her bare feet, and could glare back at him almost on an even keel. 'I'm Molly Patterson, not some floozie you picked up in the village. If you think I don't understand, then tell me!'

His glare gradually faded, but the pain did not. 'I said she had congenital hearing loss,' he sighed, his face distorted with pain. 'It has something to do with her inherited genes. It doesn't run in *my* family, and it doesn't run in *Susan's* family. Dear God, Molly, I love that child with all my heart. Susan is her mother, I'm positive of that. I was there when she was born. But I wish the hell I knew who her father was!'

An hour later, snug in bed, Molly wrestled with the problem. He didn't come back because I'm pretty, she told herself. And he didn't come back because I'm rich—I think. He came back because of the money, and because he needed help with his daughter. And that's the way I have to play it. Best friend, that's my role again. Don't be too sombre, girl, and for heaven's sake don't weep over him! Be cool, be calm, be normal. Argue with him, fight with him, laugh with him—but don't ever let him know how much you love him!

And as for the little girl—whose daughter was she? Had Susan become that much of a tramp that a man wouldn't know his own child? A dear lovable little girl with a handicap. So how to approach the problem? First of all, accept the idea that Moira *is* his daughter. Secondly, make no great show about her handicap. Treat her as a normal healthy child. Avoid embarrassing her. Speak slowly, clearly but unobtrusively. And do everything you can to build up the child's confidence against the impending wall of silence that threatens her!

And with all her thoughts thought, all her plans planned, Molly turned over on her side and tried to sleep. It was difficult. Just on the other side of that wall is Tim Holland, she told herself fiercely, the man that I'm not going to give another emotional thought to. And oh, how I want him!

CHAPTER TWO

MOLLY was busy at her dressing-table at seven the next morning, brushing her shining hair, when little Moira knocked and walked in. 'How about that?' smiled Molly. She was wearing a pink flannel nightgown which stretched from high-buttoned neckline to her ankles, caressing her curves as it fell. Moira, wearing one of Molly's old shirts over her stick-figure, managed to achieve the same general appearance, the tails of the shirt reaching down to her ankles. The child climbed up on to the bench beside Molly, squirmed a bit, and looked into the mirror.

'Whatcha doing?' she queried.

'Braiding my hair. I prefer to keep it out of the way, and yet I don't have the courage to get it cut. Don't you braid yours? It's certainly long enough.'

'No.'

'Just no?' Molly put her brush down and looked at the child's mirror-reflection. A very stubborn little chin was tilted slightly upward to emphasise her determination.

'Just no. I don't like to show my ears.'

'But you have very pretty ears, Moira.'

'Kids laugh at me when they see my hearing aid. Ears ain't pretty when you have to stuff them with 'lectric.'

Oh my, Molly sighed to herself. Here we go! A child's peers can be the most cruel people in the world. Anybody *different* is to be mocked! And now what, Miss Patterson?

'Look at me, Moira,' she ordered. The child responded, looking straight ahead into the mirror. Molly leaned to

28

one side and opened a drawer. Her gold wire-rimmed glasses came to hand. She took them out, cleaned them casually with a Kleenex, and slipped them on. 'There,' she said in a very satisfied tone. 'Don't they look nice?'

'They do,' the child returned. 'But you wasn't wearing them last night. How come?'

'That's because I was too stupid,' Molly explained. 'I think they look ugly. But if I don't wear them, I can't see.'

'You can't see?' The child's interest was immense. 'Nothing?'

'Well, I can see shapes,' Molly admitted. 'And when people stand really close I can make them out. But only just barely.'

'That's stupid all right,' Moira agreed. 'You *hafta* see. Only a dummy wouldn't wear glasses when she can't see. And besides, they're kind of cute!'

'Yes, well, maybe they are,' Molly said reflectively. 'And of course, people who can't hear are dummies if they don't wear their hearing aids, and besides, I think they look cute!'

'Why, I——' The little girl stammered to a stop and then sat quietly for a moment. 'That was a trick, wasn't it?' she said softly. Molly looked down at her. The child had disappeared, to be replaced by the tiny adult again. How old could she really be?

'Not exactly. I was thinking more of a bargain.'

Silence. And then, very cautiously, 'What kind of bargain?'

'I figure that I'll wear my glasses just as long as you wear your hearing aid, and we'll both be proud of ourselves no matter what anybody says, because we'll both know we're cute!'

And now let's see if the fish will bite at the lure, Molly thought, as she continued her braiding. I *want* her to bite.

I want very much to see this little girl happy. I want to help her to know as she goes down the tunnel into silence that there are many other ways to communicate with the world. I *want* her to be happy! I've only known her for twenty-four hours, and I don't understand why I should care so much, but I do!

'How do you do this braiding stuff?' Moira interrupted her train of thought. The child was twisting her hair as best she could, with no good result. Two pairs of eyes met in the mirror, and a conspiratorial smile was exchanged.

Tim was the last one down for breakfast, but after all, it was Saturday. Sleep had erased the haunted look from his face. His daughter was a ray of sunshine, her hair in two proud braids down her back as she helped Molly with the breakfast preparations. Which was fortunate, because the weather was all fog and grey outside the windows.

'But it can't get in!' Moira said shrilly. Now that Molly was aware, she noticed the occasional flatness of tone when the girl spoke, a sure indication that the child could not clearly hear herself.

'No, it can't get in.' Molly smiled gently at Tim and automatically reached for the eggs. He was a big man, she remembered. He favoured ham and eggs and toast and coffee and orange juice, and could occasionally be tempted towards steak and eggs. But he burned it off as fast as he took it in.

Molly searched him out surreptitiously as she worked. His thatch-coloured hair had receded just the tiniest bit on the right side of his head, where he combed it. It was as unruly as always, but he had taken the time to shave and comb and wash, and looked very much as he had years ago. Except for the two deep furrows on his forehead, and a tiny scar just at the side of his patrician nose. There might be just a fleck of white in his hair—just the tiniest speck. It gave him a more distinguished look, she thought as she rescued the eggs and slid them on to a plate. His blue eyes were clear and warm this morning, his oval face considerably thinner than once it had been. But, altogether Tim. She sighed a gusty appreciation as she filled the plate and put it on the table in front of him.

'How come *you* make the breakfast here?' Moira looked up at her with a happy grin on her face. 'My dad makes breakfast at home, you know.'

'Not when there's a woman around,' Tim teased.

'That's the way it is, Moira,' Molly sighed sombrely. 'Woman's work is never done. You should have been born a boy.'

'Not me,' the child responded quickly. 'Girls are nicer. Boys are all whiskers and dirty shoes and toads!'

'Funny,' laughed Molly as she took her own plate to the table and sat down, 'it took me twenty-five years to discover that, and here you know it all already? When's your birthday?' The child must be nearly eight, she was so grown up.

'Mapril,' Moira pronounced solemnly.

'That's certainly a nice month for a birthday,' Molly agreed cautiously.

'Yes. It's flexible,' her father interjected. 'We're always moved around a great deal, and——'

'I understand,' Molly returned. Vagabonds, she thought sympathetically. They may have had a happy life, but they have no roots! 'My, we have a lot of things to do today,' she added.

'We have?' They both spoke in startled unison.

'We have,' she maintained firmly. 'There's going to be a great deal of running around, what with this new arrangement. I need to get a better car.'

'But you ain't got no——'

'Don't have a——' her father corrected quickly. 'This child doesn't quite have a speaking acquaintance with English.' He patted the little girl on her head, then softened the blow. 'But her French is pretty good, and her Spanish is excellent.' His hand played lovingly with Moira's braids.

'But you don't have a car.' Moira re-stated her proposition. 'I looked outside. All you got—all you have is a bicycle.'

'You just didn't look in the barn behind the house,' Molly chided. 'I have a car. Well, maybe that's too strong a word—it's not much of a car. But that makes it all the easier for me to buy a better car, doesn't it?' She sniffed disdainfully as the pair of them stared at her.

'Female logic,' Tim declaimed pompously. 'Come to think of it, your Aunt Molly always did follow a twisted path in reasoning.'

'I don't understand, Daddy.'

'Chauvinist,' Molly muttered under her breath.

'That's what I said,' he chuckled. 'Eat your breakfast. What kind of a car do you want, Molly?'

'A two-door red one,' she replied, toying with her own eggs. Over the course of the last years she had become a non-breakfast eater, subsisting on innumerable cups of coffee until lunchtime, but now she felt the need to share.

'That's all your requirement?'

She glared at his grin, feeling more at home now that she and Tim were off in one of their continuing arguments.

'Of course that's all,' she said slowly, accentuating every word so even the stupid might hear. 'What more would I want? I like a two-door car because you can put little people in the back without worrying that they'll get out of the doors. I want a red one so people can see me coming. What else?'

'What about horse-power and brakes and steering?'

'What about it?' She got up to clear the dishes. 'I only want it to go. I don't care how *much* it goes. If it stops going I'll just find some man who knows all about things like that and I'll bat my eyes at him, and he'll fix it. You taking notes, Moira? Like this.'

She knelt down beside the girl's chair and slowly fluttered her eyelids. The little girl chortled and tried an imitation.

'All right now,' Tim objected, 'Don't start teaching my daughter that sort of thing!'

Molly dissolved in laughter, and almost dropped the plates. Luckily they were ironware, the sort that just won't break when dropped. Moira followed her over to the sink with a couple of saucers. One slipped out of her hand and splattered into a thousand pieces. Shag, who had been lying in the corner, got up slowly and stalked indignantly out of the way.

'Oh my!' said the child, and ducked her head. Molly tilted her chin back up with one finger.

'I never did like that saucer anyway,' she said distinctly. Moira smiled back up at her. Beamed, rather. A connection had been established.

The rain had stopped and the fog had cleared by the time they started out on their shopping trip. A little weather warning, Molly explained to the child. 'Yesterday it was chilly, today started out with rain—before we know it we'll be up to our briskets in snow. Cape Ann is not the kindest place in the winter world.'

'Where's my brisket?' She knows and she's teasing me, Molly decided. Score one for our side. She's more like her dad than ever I thought!

'Oh, that's the place just above the part that you sit on,' she explained solemnly, then stole a look and caught the little smile as she drove down through the village and along Hesperus Avenue, heading for the big city. This child is older and smarter than she ought to be, Molly thought. Seven and a half, going on eight? All her front adult teeth are in; she understands a great deal more than her father gives her credit for. This is getting to be like a Dorothy L. Sayers novel; there are mysteries within mysteries, and I'd better pay some attention to my driving!

There was not much need to choose a subject for conversation. Hesperus Avenue ran just inland from the coast, through an avenue of trees, most of them stripped of their leaves. But there was enough green cover to fill out a beautiful bucolic picture. That was, until Moira, peering out of the window to her right, spotted the twin towers of Hammond Castle. The sight shook her out of her reserve.

'A real castle, Aunt Molly!' she gasped in surprise.

'Well, not exactly real,' laughed Molly. 'Not if you mean as in knights in armour and medieval maidens, and all that. It was built by John Hammond as his home, back in the late 1920s. Mr Hammond was the inventor of FM radio. We'll come and see round it some day.'

'That's a promise?' the little girl asked wistfully. She sounded as if promises were not much kept in her short life, Molly thought, and a little pain struck her at the thought. She was quiet as they turned into Western Avenue, and thus around the western harbour and down into the centre of Gloucester.

Molly might have had some trouble buying the car she wanted. Two salesmen were prepared to give her some

argument until she mustered the magic words, 'For cash.'
So she and Moira drove away in less than an hour in a
little red four-wheel-drive Bronco 11, heading back
towards Magnolia.

'And here we are,' she smiled as she parked on
Lexington Avenue in the village.

'Yes,' the child returned doubtfully as she squirmed out
of the high seat and looked cautiously up and down the
single block of stores that marked the village centre. 'I
thought you said we were going to the shopping area.'

'Believe it,' grinned Molly as she slid out on to the
pavement. 'This is it—the finest block of stores in
Magnolia. In fact, the *only* block of stores in Magnolia.
Shag, guard the car!'

The dog made a magnificent defender as he sat up on
the front seat and let his heavy muzzle hang over the side
of the open window. Strangers walking down the road
veered away at the sight of him, not knowing that he was
a spiritual brother of Ferdinand the Bull.

And so the two went, hand in hand, like the best of
friends, down to Ina's to find something to suit the child.
Another surprise for Molly: little Miss Holland knew
exactly what she wanted, and got it. Jeans that met the
modern style; dresses that both fitted and were attractive.
And underwear. And how Moira revelled in the
underwear department!

The last stop on the trip was the Star Market, out on
Route 1A, where numberless sacks of groceries required
the help of one of the bag boys, and the little car was
comfortably full.

'It must of cost a lot,' Moira commented ruefully as
she tried to find a space to sit.

'You don't want to know,' Molly answered firmly.
'Sufficient unto the day is the evil thereof. That's from

the Bible. I'm not sure what it means.'

'You know what it means,' the little girl—suddenly adult again—said. 'You know everything. You can fool my daddy, but you can't fool me.' Her little head cocked to one side as she studied her new aunt solemnly.

'Have you been in love with him for a long time?'

'In love with whom?' asked Molly, stalling for time.

'With my dad,' the girl sighed in exasperation.

'Bite your tongue,' Molly muttered savagely, and ground the gears as she headed back to the house.

He was waiting for them outside under the grape arbour when they drove up. Proud of herself and her car, Molly applied the brakes a little too strongly, and skidded to a halt in a cloud of dust and pebbles.

'Hiyo, Silver.' Tim touched a finger to the brim of his hat in a sort of salute as he leaned over into the car. 'Red. It certainly is red!'

'Unnecessarily smart remarks will leave you without lunch,' Molly snapped. 'There are packages to be carried.'

'And I suppose I'm the *carrier*?' He tilted his hat back on his head and grinned.

'Was there any doubt?' she answered primly. 'Why else would any sensible woman want a man around the house?'

'Why indeed?' he agreed as he lifted his daughter out from between all the packages.

'Don't forget carrying out the garbage,' the young lady interjected. 'That's another thing men are good for.'

'I can see this is going to be a hard winter,' Tim laughed as he set the girl down on the ground, pointed her towards the house, and patted her bottom to urge her on.

They both watched as the child skipped towards the

house. Shag, ambling along beside her, looked to be twice as large as Moira, and his ancient tail was wagging in time with her gabbing. Molly stiffened as Tim's arm came around her shoulder, then she forced herself to relax. He hardly seemed to notice.

'Buy anything besides the car?' he teased.

'Groceries,' she said very firmly. 'We have to eat.'

'Yes, and I expect to pay for the eating,' he replied.

'I don't——' she started.

'But I do,' he interrupted. His strong hand squeezed her shoulder, and a little shiver ran up her spine. 'How much do you think you'll need for a month?'

His hand moved away as he fished in the pocket of his jeans for his wallet. She missed the warmth of it instantly. 'I haven't the faintest idea, Tim. I've never budgeted for a fam—for a group, before. I've got plenty of money. Let's let it run for a month and then we can square accounts.'

'You're sure?' Those dark blue eyes stared into her green ones. 'This place doesn't look all *that* prosperous.'

'I'm not a charity case,' she snapped. 'Don't judge by the amount of painting that needs to be done. That's because you can't hire a house-painter for any amount of money these days!'

'Hey, whoa!' Both hands were back on her indignant shoulders. 'I'm not trying to insult you, Molly. So you're doing well. I'm glad for you. And whatever it is you want, we'll do it *your* way.'

She came back down to earth with a thump. Why in the world should I get angry with Tim about money? she thought. Or about anything, for that matter? He's a good man. Just because he can't see beyond the end of his nose there's no reason for me to cloud up and storm all over him! And his daughter is a lovely child, and it's going to be a long cold winter, and I'm lucky to have the company, aren't I?

'Yes, well—I'm sorry I snapped at you,' she sighed. 'And I can't ever remember you giving up an argument so easily. Now, how about moving the groceries?'

'After we have a small talk, away from prying ears,' he coaxed. That warm arm came around her shoulders again. But it's only friendship, she warned herself. He doesn't really think about me as a—female. She gritted her teeth and moved at his urging, out under the grape arbour that hugged the south side of the house.

'Picked every single grape, I see,' mused Tim, and her temper flared. This wasn't what she wanted to talk about!

'No such thing,' she snapped, then relented. Dear lord, he was Tim, not some bum like Alfred DeMoins. So maybe he was blind, but—the thought brought a little smile to her face as she readjusted her glasses. 'No,' she said more softly. 'I left everything on the vine until after the first frost. That's what the Germans do, you know. It improves the wine. They call it *spätlese*. Only a flock of starlings ganged up on me. There must have been over a hundred of them, and they stripped the arbour in two days, before the frost could come. Now, what was it you wanted to talk about?'

'Over here,' he said, and guided her to the end of the arbour, and the crooked-legged old bench that *he* had built for her when she was eleven years old. He patted it affectionately. Molly pulled her coat closer around her and settled back.

'It's about Moira and you and me,' he said, joining her on the rough planks. The short leg dipped under his weight and she slid the inch or two down the incline that put her thigh hard up against his. Not a bad start, she told herself as she made an effort to move an inch away. Moira first, and I'm second. Or better still, I'm in the middle, between Moira and Tim. That's nice. But it's only a dream.

'I'm listening,' she urged. The sun was up and full, shining every bit of power it had on the south side of the house. But still, it was late November, and although old Sol was doing its best it was a bleak effort. A little shiver ran down her spine as Tim draped one arm casually around her shoulders.

'I want you to understand,' he said softly. 'In everything I do, Moira comes first. I need a great deal of money to be sure that *she* goes first-class. If I can't buy her a cure, I *can* buy her a comfortable life.'

'I understand, Tim.' Almost unconsciously her head tilted sideways and landed on his broad shoulder.

'So, for the next three or four months I'm going to play shark in the money sea, Molly. It'll take me all hours of the day and night. I expect it will throw me in with some strange bedfellows, and I know I'll have to skirt the edges of some laws—from your viewpoint, I suppose it might even occasionally look like a dirty pool. But I'm going to do it.'

It was a great deal to think about, and Molly could hardly reason past 'strange bedfellows'. Only a cliché, of course, but it struck her at a vulnerable point. 'You mustn't go so far that she won't recognise who you are,' she returned. 'It wouldn't be much fun discovering that your father is a shark—even if a civilised one.'

'You object?' Cold, bitter words, almost as if he had bitten each one before he spat it out.

'I don't object, Tim,' she said firmly. 'I don't have the right to object. Just tell me what you want me to do about Moira.'

'A great deal,' he offered, squeezing her shoulder. 'I

want you to mother her for me until springtime.'

'Mother her? Almost any woman could do that.'

'That's not true,' he grumbled. 'Lord knows I've tried enough different types of women to do just that, and none of them was a success. Moira's been battered from pillar to post—mentally, that is—from the number of substitute mothers she's had.'

And there I go, Molly told herself glumly. Just the current substitute, in a long line of women. I'd like to hit him right on his nose—if I dared.

'I think I can tell you your biggest mistake,' she said cautiously. He cocked his head and looked down at her.

'If you'd selected a woman *just* to be Moira's mother you wouldn't have had all those problems. But I'll bet you couldn't leave it at that, Tim. You had to drag them into your bed, didn't you!'

'Hey,' he objected, 'cool down!' He had a temper of his own, as well she remembered. Molly moved away from him an inch or two. 'No, I didn't *drag* any of them into my bed. But I sure had a tough time keeping them *out* of it.' One of his fists banged into the other as he took out his frustration on himself. 'What I need is a motherly person who doesn't look at me as a sex object!' Again that fist slapping into the palm of his hand. Molly's heart fell clear through her boots.

'But you don't really know anything about me, Tim,' she protested weakly. 'I haven't been sitting here on this bench for all those years just waiting for you to pop up!'

'Hey, I know all about you,' he grinned. 'All about how you grew up—and out—and got your degree, and won the state's Teacher of the Year Award for being the best Special Education teacher——'

'Twice in a row,' she interjected, thinking, well, it's not often that a girl gets to blow her own horn!

'Twice in a row?' He squeezed her gently. 'Aunt Gerda forgot that part.'

'Ah, Aunt Gerda.' Molly grinned. 'The Great Seer, who sees all, knows all, tells all—and the only decent human being in the Holland family!'

'You've got the lady just right,' he agreed. 'She's been writing to me once a month, through all these years. And in fact she——' He stopped, looking like a man whose tongue has just overrun his common sense.

'In fact she what?' she demanded.

He shrugged his shoulders and gave her that lopsided grin which, she knew from experience, signified that he didn't intend to say another word on *that* subject.

'Funny,' Molly mused, 'I've heard a lot from your aunt Gerda too. In fact, I've been down to her place in Framingham a few times, when I needed a refuge.'

'Oh? Refuge? That's something she never mentioned.'

'Well, thank the lord for that!' sighed Molly. 'But anyway, you were talking to Aunt Gerda, and she said something, and that's when you thought about Molly Patterson,' she stated challengingly.

'And that's when I thought of Molly Patterson,' he agreed. 'Will you fill in for me until springtime?'

Yes, certainly, she wanted to say. I'll be glad to mother your daughter. But I'm not saying that, some time in the dark of winter, I might not poison you, Tim Holland. Or dump you in boiling oil, or push you off the cliffs! Damn you, man, can't you see what's in front of your eyes?

She struggled with herself, her back turned quickly in his direction to mask the anguish. Her voice was perceptibly weaker as she turned around again. 'And after springtime, then what?' It was a question she *had* to ask, but didn't want to. Or rather it was the *answer* that she didn't want to hear.

'After that, I suppose we'll have to reassess the situation,' Tim said sombrely. 'Is that asking too much, friend Molly?'

'No, lord, no.' She hurried her answer, wanting to get it in before he had a change of mind. 'But you know that in every family there has to be discipline?'

'I'll take care of that part,' he said grimly. 'You just do the happiness bit; I'll do the rest. And I pay all the expenses. You won't be able to do whatever you usually do for a living.'

'I'm a schoolteacher by trade,' she reminded him. 'But, as they say in the theatre, I'm resting at the moment.'

'So I'll throw in a salary too,' he insisted. Molly squirmed around on the seat, reached up, and pulled his stubborn chin around.

'I'm doing this for friendship, Tim Holland,' she declared angrily. 'If I were doing it for money, you couldn't afford me.'

'Hey, take it easy, Moll! I just thought——'

'Remember the time you and Jackie ruined my best doll?' she asked ominously as she struggled out of his grasp and stood up in front of him.

'Well now,' he drawled, a big smile on his face, 'as I remember, you got Jackie down and kicked one of his teeth out, and then you——'

'How would you like *another* black eye, Timothy Holland?' she interrupted, balling up her fist in front of his nose.

He was up, locking her fist in one capable hand, before she could catch a breath. Somehow or another both his hands moved to her shoulders, then around her back as he pulled her hard up against him. 'And do *you* remember what happened right after that?' he whispered in her ear.

'I don't recall,' she maintained angrily as she struggled

to escape his grasp.

'Try this on for size,' he muttered, and his warm, moist lips were on hers, drawing her out from herself. His tongue probed at her, and she could feel the surge of tingling emotion that spread out from her midriff into every portion of her body. For a long minute Tim crushed her to him, as eager as any swain could be. For a long moment the sky behind her closed eyelids flashed with rocket explosions. Then he put her gently away.

'I—don't remember anything like that,' she gasped as she leaned her head under his chin.

'No,' he agreed, and there was an odd tone to his voice, 'I don't remember it being just exactly that way either.' Molly couldn't see his face, or the puzzled expression that flitted across his brow.

'What was you two doing out there all that time?' Moira enquired as her father brought in the last of the groceries.

'Talking,' Tim returned. 'Grown-up talk.'

'It sure didn't look like talking,' his daughter giggled. 'Although it was pretty hard to see clearly from the kitchen window. I had to climb up on a chair to see out the top part! Aunt Molly, did you know your windows were that dirty?'

'How would you like to clean them all?' her father threatened. 'All we need around these parts is a little snoop! Help your aunt put the groceries away!'

'You gotta help,' the little girl laughed as she dodged him by running around the table. 'Molly's making lunch, and I can't reach all the shelves, so you'll——'

'Oh, great,' he grumbled as he set to work. The pair of them made a game of it. Molly, whipping up an egg salad for luncheon sandwiches, followed them with her eyes and felt just a little twinge of jealousy.

Moira should have been *my* daughter, she told herself as she took down a can of soup and began warming it. What a fine family we'd make! There, I said it—well, at least I thought it. Family! But why am I getting so—angry? I've been a day late and a dollar short all through my life. I wonder if I'm too late to strangle Susan? Come to think of it, he never mentioned if they were divorced!

As a result of her little conversation with herself she thumped the plates down on the table in front of the pair of them, and managed to spill more than a little of the mushroom soup on to Tim's lap.

'Hey, that's hot!' he protested. His daughter glared at him, and probably kicked him under the table, Molly thought, because he swallowed the rest of his protests, manufactured an injured smile, and picked up his spoon.

'My fault,' Molly admitted. 'I was thinking about something, and——'

'Something bad?' Moira squirmed in her seat, those brown eyes tracking Molly's every move.

'Well, for a fact,' said Molly, 'it was something rather nice. I thought I was strangling my worst enemy!'

'Ooh——'

'Hush up, baby,' her father interjected. 'It might have been me she was thinking about. Or you.'

'Never you, Moira.' But Molly was not about to offer any soothing for Tim, and his quick mind caught it up instantly. The rest of the meal passed in comparative safety, as Moira told him, in excruciating detail, about their morning shopping trip.

'And then there was this castle, Dad.' The little girl was full of life as she did her best to describe it all. Until, at the end, 'Aunt Molly, did you ever dream about bein' a princess and livin' in a castle?'

Caught unawares, Molly blushed. What to answer? Certainly not the truth. Tell her yes, but my knight ran off with the other woman? 'I hadn't given it much thought,' she lied brightly. But Tim's eyes were following her, staring, questioning. She shrugged her shoulders.

'Your aunt Molly was always a practical person,' Tim told his daughter. 'She didn't have much time for that romantic stuff.'

'And you believe that . . .?' his daughter sighed.

Tim waited around downstairs, remembering that little remark, until the two females went up 'to make the beds', Molly had said. When he was sure they were out of sight he picked up the telephone. The Framingham number was engraved on his mind, so he had no need for a book. And his aunt Gerda answered on the second ring.

'Tim? I hadn't expected to hear from you so quickly, nephew. Well?'

'I'm not sure that it's all that well, Gerda,' he replied softly. 'We're in—the pair of them are upstairs housekeeping. Molly has taken to Moira, I can see that.'

'I told you she would,' the chief schemer of the Holland family told him. 'A real softy, Molly Patterson is.'

'Maybe,' he sighed. 'About kids and dogs and lost causes. But I'm not so sure that Tim Holland rates on her list any more. I've tried a couple of—well, they didn't work out at all. She's bound and determined to be my best friend—and that's all. I can see that written all over her face every time I try to get too close.'

'Early days yet,' his aunt advised. 'You can't expect to recover all the ground you've lost in ten years, Timothy. I told you and told you what a fool you were being, but you wouldn't listen, would you? Well, now you'll just have to play it my way.'

'I wish I were as sure as you are,' he admitted. 'She's

just as lovely and desirable and warm as ever she was before, and I'm having a hard time *not* telling her—or keeping my hands off her. Are you sure, Aunt Gerda?'

'I'm sure,' his aunt replied. 'Just remember all the experience I've had.' For the life of him, Tim had trouble recalling. His aunt Gerda had contracted a young and foolish marriage, and only the quick death of the man she had chosen had kept him from running through her entire inheritance. Two years of wedded non-bliss. Did that qualify her as an expert? But then, considering how poorly he had done for himself, Tim shrugged his shoulders. Anybody in the world could know more about love and marriage than Tim Holland did. His one encounter with Susan had shaken his confidence about women completely.

'Well, all right,' he agreed reluctantly. 'I'll keep it up. Slow and easy wins the race?'

'Propinquity, that's what does it,' his aunt assured him. 'Keep your mouth shut and your ears open, and be noticeable. Got it? Now hang up before she gets suspicious! And next time, call me from a phone booth. When she gets her monthly bill she'll see this call listed, idiot!'

'Yes—yes, ma'am,' he replied, but his aunt had already hung up. He put the instrument down, feeling about as unsure a conspirator as Brutus must have been the night before Julius Caesar was murdered!

CHAPTER THREE

GLOUCESTER, with some twenty-seven thousand inhabitants, is neither the largest nor the oldest city in Massachusetts, yet it has always had an important place in the scheme of things. It huddles around the shallow waters of Gloucester harbour, protected from the harsh Atlantic by Eastern Point. Like many Yankee cities, it is surrounded by others: Essex, Rockport, Manchester-by-the-Sea. And it incorporates the tiny village of Magnolia, like bait at the end of a long fishing line. The city sits by the sea, and draws its life from the fishing fleet. Not a deepwater fleet, such as home ports like New Bedford, but rather the inshore fleet, the smaller boats. Fishing is an industry that has been sick for years, and Gloucester looks it.

The two of them, Moira and Molly, had made the short trip up the shore road again, wandered through the maze of streets in the centre, and finally parked illegally on Pleasant Street, across from St Agnes. The church and the parish school, that was. For some reason it all looks smaller than it did, Molly thought as she scanned the old building. And older. Can it really be twenty years since Tim and I both went to school here? Dear lord!

'It's sort of scary.' Moira, her happy chatter overawed, clutched at Molly's hand and moved closer. 'I wish my dad could of come.'

'Could have,' Molly agreed. 'And your dad was up and out of the house by seven o'clock. You have to keep up your self-confidence, Moira. All the people in this building are nice people, and they all want to help. Besides, your dad is down in Beantown now, wrestling with the bears of Wall Street.'

'Bears? I thought he was in the fishing business?' The little head cocked to one side as the child looked up at her. Watch your tongue, Molly warned herself. She's smarter than you are!

'It's just an old phrase people use when they talk about the Stock Market.' She fumbled for a better explanation as she led Moira in through the double doors and down the corridor to the Principal's office. 'You should have seen how scared *I* was when my mother brought me here. But Tim—your father—was already enrolled, so——'

'And so you were both the nicest students in the school?'

Molly almost choked. 'Er—yes, of course,' she lied heartily. 'We—were the very model of outstanding students. Yes, your father and I—well!'

Sister Alice was standing at her open door as they came around the corner. The elderly lady, barely five feet tall, plump, spry, with the marks of forty years of teaching on her face, was dressed in a serviceable brown street dress, with a wooden cross suspended around her neck on a leather thong. She put out both her hands towards Molly.

'I'm sure you don't remember me,' Molly started to say, when the nun began to laugh, then covered her mouth with one hand as she waved them both into her office.

'Molly Patterson,' Sister mused as she settled into the big chair behind the desk. 'I knew it had to be Molly Patterson. I was looking out of the window when you got out of your car, and the moment I saw that hair——Well, little Molly, all grown up, and bringing your daughter to us?'

'Er—not exactly,' Molly sputtered. 'I—I don't

suppose you remember Timmy Holland? I——'

'Of course,' the nun chuckled. 'The Terrible Duo. How could I forget?'

'You knew my dad?' Moira's reserve was overcome by the magic word—dad. She wriggled off her chair and went over to the desk. 'He came to this school too?'

'So—Tim Holland's girl. Come around here to the light and let me get a good look at you.' Sister Alice swivelled her chair around and took Moira's little face between her hands. 'Why, of course. I knew your dad, and——'

'Aunt Molly,' the child prompted.

'Aunt Molly, is it?' Sister Alice suppressed a sigh. 'I would have bet a fortune that Tim and Molly would have married. Lucky I'm not a betting woman!' The old hands gently caressed the child's blonde hair. 'Always in trouble, that pair. Your father was the ringleader, but he never realised that Molly's hair stood out a mile in any direction. Any time there was a commotion that head of red-gold hair could be seen, standing out in the crowd like a lighthouse. We always knew right away who the culprits were!'

'Trouble?' Moira looked astonished. 'Molly said they was—they were perfect students!'

Sister Alice rang a little hand-bell on her desk and squirmed back in her chair, her tiny feet dangling, unable to reach the floor. 'I've always meant to get this chair lowered,' the nun commented. 'But then I thought it was a temporary job, so—yes, of course,' she agreed amiably. 'Perfect students, your father and your aunt. Yes, I recall that now.'

A senior girl student came in from the Administrative office. 'Althea,' the Principal said gently, 'this is——' she looked down at the paper that Molly had placed in the middle of the desk '——Moira Holland, who is considering entering our school. Would you show her around the building while her mother—I beg your pardon—while her aunt and I have a talk?'

Moira went reluctantly, holding the hand of her preceptor, and looking back over her shoulder appealingly at Molly. 'Now then,' Sister Alice said briskly, 'to business. You said on the telephone that she was a special interest child?'

'She has a hearing problem,' said Molly. 'One ear is totally deaf, in the other she requires a hearing aid about which she's very sensitive. She reads lips excellently.' All that was said gently, and then, unable to control her thoughts, 'It's a degenerative disease, Sister. I'm afraid there's no cure. I hope we can—damn! Excuse me, Sister, I seem to have gotten something in my eye.'

'Yes, I can see that,' the nun replied. 'I seem to have a problem myself. Degenerative?'

'Yes. Hereditary.'

'Does she know?'

'Yes, she knows. And seems so light-hearted about it all that I suspect she's all bundled up inside.'

'And may break down or out at any time,' the Principal mused.

'She might,' Molly sighed, 'but before it all happens, she needs to mix with others, to build up a larger vocabulary, to become adjusted to her peers. And I intend to teach her sign language!'

'And who better?' Sister commented. 'Now that I recall, there was something in the newspapers a year or more ago about you, Molly Patterson. Would you tell me something if I ask an impertinent question?'

'I suppose I would,' Molly said softly. Even though I don't know anything more about Moira, I suppose there may be something I forgot! But when the question came, it left her completely off course.

'Why is it that you and Timmy never married?'

'I——' Molly stood up stiffly, stared out of the windows and around the room before coming back to the smooth sweet face of the nun. 'I suppose,' she stammered, 'because he never asked me!'

'Well, I don't see Moira as a problem,' Sister replied after a long pause for reflection. 'Of course, we expect the parents to interest themselves in the school's work——'

'Timmy—oh dear,' Molly sighed. 'She hasn't a mother, you see——'

'I see perfectly,' the old nun chuckled. 'So Timmy Holland just brought her home and dumped her on you? Times haven't changed a bit!'

'It's not *exactly* like that,' Molly objected, then shrugged her shoulders as Sister Alice stared her down. 'Well yes, it's exactly like that. And there are more problems. They've been living in France, and the child has been educated——' She fumbled for the right word.

'Haphazardly?'

'The very word.' The two women smiled at each other. 'There aren't any school records. I have no idea what grade she would fit into. She's going to be eight very soon, but I——'

'No problem,' Sister assured her. 'We'll test her, then make an assignment. She's a lovely child. Behaviour problems?'

'Not that I know of,' Molly answered, then added, 'Well, she's very reserved. That's a tendency of children who are hard of hearing. And then you have to remember that she *is* Timmy's daughter, you know. I would suppose she——'

The Principal swung back and forth in her chair for a

moment, to work up momentum, then got to her feet, laughing. 'I understand entirely,' she smiled. 'She's Tim Holland's daughter and Molly Patterson is her aunt, and everyone knows that *they* were perfect students! But there is a price to pay, you know.'

'The tuition? I—Sister Alice, Tim doesn't know that I've brought Moira here, and I don't think he has—well, I suspect he has money problems. I'll pay for everything.'

'Of course there's that,' Sister sighed. 'And it gets more expensive every day. But that's not exactly what I meant, you know.'

'Then what?' Molly's brain raced through all the things she knew about St Agnes, and none of them added up to extremely high fees. The smile on the Sister Superior's face was too broad to be passed up.

'No, no,' Sister said. 'We require parents to participate in the school's activities. Usually it turns out to be the mother—or the aunt, if that applies. Especially if the aunt is the best Special Needs teacher in Massachusetts. It would be wonderful, Molly, if you might see your way clear to teach a class in sign language once a week?'

'Why, I—I didn't know you had that many handicapped,' Molly started to say, but the Principal held up a hand to stop her.

'If you mean physically handicapped,' she said softly, 'we have our share. But that's not what I have in mind. We need to sensitise our non-handicapped children to the needs of others, and learning sign language would be the ideal way. We can't afford to pay for a teacher of your calibre, Molly. Could you see your way clear to——'

'Of course,' Molly interrupted. 'Of course I could.' Soft-hearted Molly, she told herself. Everybody walks on Molly. But then when she looked up, Sister Alice was smiling so broadly, so warmly, that she realised immediately that one hour a week could hardly compare with the sacrifices that this tiny nun was making in *her* life.

Molly was still blushing as she drove home, leaving Moira behind for the day. A skein of high thin clouds had closed over the area, shutting out the sun. With that, the temperature was dropping fast. She detoured through the waterfront. Gulls were coming ashore to roost on the flat roofs of buildings, a sure sign that a storm was coming. A pair of fishing boats, their rigging heavily hung with ice, were doggedly ploughing up the channel. Molly shook her head. A hard way to make a living, fishing.

They were both home at Magnolia at six o'clock. Moira camped out on the living-room floor for a cartoon session in front of the television set. But Molly had the need for fresh air, for solitude, a chance to think. She slipped on her Fair Isle sweater under her heavy coat and strolled out in the twilight to the edge of the bluff.

Some long-ago Patterson had built a little wooden gazebo here at the edge of the cliff. With rails instead of walls, and a roof to keep off the weather, it provided the perfect observation post. From its north side a pair of haphazardly constructed wooden stairs zig-zagged their way down the cliff to the little patch of sandy beach where one or two boats could be tied up. Directly at her feet to the east, looking out over the Atlantic Ocean, were the three rocky islands that marked the entrance to Kettle Cove. A tiny boat, no longer than thirty feet, was re-setting lobster-pots in the cover itself, rushing to beat the knell of darkness.

Two immense stone crocks which once had held flowers guarded each side of the landward entrance to the gazebo. The flowers had long since gone and now the crocks served as outdoor garbage collectors. Molly patted the side of one of them with a cold hand. Her adventurous great-uncle Bill had brought them both back from Egypt at great cost as mementoes of the great Pharaonic culture, only to discover they had been manufactured in Brooklyn. But the Patterson family had always been like that; enthusiastic after causes, with perhaps too much warm-heartedness.

The skyscraper lights of Boston splashed a brilliant fluorescence into the darkling sky in competition with the cool winter moon that sat on the sea-horizon. With the coming of sunset the wind was preparing to shift, and for a moment a quiet calm lay over the bay and the headlands. The headlights of the Porsche outlined Molly as Tim drove up to the house. In a moment he was at her side.

Molly turned slightly to welcome him. He smiled back as he came up alongside and laid an arm around her shoulders. She barely suppressed the sigh of contentment, and leaned back against him, enjoying the clean warmth and strength. 'There's been a shortage of men for leaning on in these parts lately.' She rubbed her head gently into his shoulder, and the sigh escaped.

'Aha!' he laughed. 'I knew you missed me! Where's Moira?'

And that's all the attention I'm going to get, Molly told herself as she folded her arms across her stomach and moved an inch or two away. 'In the house, watching the tube. A black and white movie. I think it's called *Godzilla Eats the World*.'

'Hey, don't knock it!' His arm pulled her so that her back was against his chest, and now one of his arms rested on each shoulder, hugging her gently. 'I think we saw that flick ourselves a good many years ago, didn't we? You were always a sucker for horror movies! How did the day go?'

Molly needed a moment to fight back all the errant little

impulses that ran up and down her spine as she relaxed against him and his hands moved down to her waist and covered her own. 'Funny you should ask,' she said primly. 'Why didn't you tell me?'

'Why didn't I tell you what?'

'That Moira has never ever been to *any* school before?'

He was so close that she could feel his warm breath at her ear, and for a second she hoped he was going to nibble on the lobe. One of her fetishes, earlobe-nibbling. A girl could hardly expect to hang around for ten years without *some* experimenting. With regret, Molly acknowledged to herself that that was as far as it ever had got. But this was Tim, and he wasn't in a nibbling mood! Which earned him another sigh.

'You enrolled her in school? It never crossed my mind to say,' he admitted. There was just the slightest bit of apology in his voice, but no interest in her sighs. 'She's had a tutor all this time. Why? What happened?'

'Well, the guidance counsellor down at St Agnes gave her a battery of tests to decide in which grade they should start her, and her reading level is already at the ninth grade, Tim! And her other scores would make you stand up and cheer. I told Sister Alice she was almost eight years old, just about right for the third grade, but they put her in the fifth! I just hope it doesn't cause her any problems.' The silence of the sea enfolded them for a moment. 'Tim?'

'I heard.' He sounded so distant that she turned slightly in his arms, but his face was masked by the rapidly gathering night. He seemed to shake himself. 'I think she'll be OK. She's not only older than you think, but she's also older than the average child of her age. I'm more concerned about how *you* got along with her, Molly.'

'Me?' She twisted out of his arms and moved away, kicking at a pebble. 'I—we get along fine,' she said. 'It's getting chilly. Maybe we'd better go have some supper?'

'Good idea.' Tim took a step or two in her direction, blocking out the moonlight. Both his hands fell on her shoulders again as he pulled her close. Mesmerised, she watched his head move closer, blocking out more and more of the sky. The light was dim, but the little scar on his nose seemed to increase the closer it came. He's going to kiss me, she reasoned with alarm, and then I'm going to fall into little pieces, and heaven knows what I'll do!

He *did* kiss her—on the tip of her patrician little nose. 'Thanks, buddy,' he murmured. He was off towards the house in a loping run before she could muster up a word. Which was probably just as well, because all the words she could think of were hardly ladylike at all.

'Buddy,' she muttered under her breath as she regained her control. 'Boy, you've got something coming to you, Tim Holland! And you're going to get it any day soon, you just watch and see!' She was still nibbling on her full lower lip when she came up the stairs and into the house.

The pair of them were sitting on the floor in front of her twenty-six inch television screen when she banged the door behind her, stopped long enough to hang her sweater on the old coat rack by the door, and went straight into the kitchen. A few minutes later the music on the television programme swelled to a finale, and the pair of them tumbled into the kitchen like a pair of frolicking bear-cubs.

'What's for supper?' Moira carolled as she appropriated the best chair. Her father took the adjoining chair and both sat looking up expectantly at Molly.

When she turned around from the serving counter with two plates in her hand, and a grim expression on her face, all the smiles disappeared. 'Cornflakes,' she muttered as she slammed a plate down in front of each of them.

'But that's breakfast——' The little girl jumped as if someone might have kicked her ankle under the table. 'I—just love cornflakes,' she added timorously. 'Don't you, Dad?'

'Love them,' he agreed nervously. 'I really love—er—cornflakes.'

'I'm glad,' muttered Molly. But then the tension grew too high, and her right eye sprang a leak. She glared at the two of them and ran for the stairs.

She slammed into her room, stalked around its perimeter while she stanched the floodtide, then threw herself down on her bed, hands clasped under her head. She stared at the ceiling with her eyes closed. Funny, that. She could still see the crack that ran across the room from corner to corner, even with her eyes closed. Superimposed on the almost white background was Tim's laughing head, with both Molly's hands wrapped around his throat as she gleefully strangled him.

Her eyes snapped open. Don't stay here, she warned herself, and bounced to her feet. You'll only feel sorry for yourself, and you know how useless a thing *that* is. Her unguided feet carried her over to the little bench in front of her vanity table. One quick hand tore loose her braids; the other snatched up her hairbrush as she punished her scalp for its—and her—transgressions. Fifty slashing strokes, until her hair sparkled and her scalp tingled. Then she put the brush down, stared into the mirror, and thought.

Pure nonsense, she lectured herself. Pure unadulterated nonsense. He caught you off guard, and there you were trying to make a mountain out of a molehill. He didn't love you ten years ago, and he doesn't love you now. He laid it all out on the line, but you, Little Miss Stupid, you have to create the world's greatest romance out of a hug, and then presume he's broken your heart just because you only got kissed on the nose! Stupid!

It's gong to be a long winter. Either you help him out, Girl Friday, according to *his* rules, or you might just as well pack up, take your money out of the bank, and go to Florida for the winter, just the way you'd originally planned. Now what's it going to be?

Out of the maze of pains all Molly's pragmatic attributes began to reassemble. She measured them one by one. So you're still stuck on Tim Holland. Poor girl. But if you play it his way, at least you'll know where he is, won't you? You'll get to see him every day, right? That's something you've not done lately. And maybe now and again he might give you a brotherly little kiss? No, don't think like that, Molly Patterson. That's a very sarcastic approach to the problem.

Think, girl! What is it that you really want? Tim Holland? Then stop being a drip, and start hunting him! Gradually, of course. Give him a little time to adjust. Then—then what? she asked herself angrily. So hunting is the female approach. It's the lioness that makes the kill, right. Just because you haven't any experience at hunting, it doesn't mean you can't learn. There are hundreds of books on the subject! Do a little better with your clothing; make him notice that you're female. Then make him jealous—how about that! Find some other man you can flaunt in Tim's face. Someone like—oh, God, Alfred?

Shaking her head, Molly leaned forward towards the mirror and inspected what she had to work with. Bright golden hair with a red tinge to it, that curled when she failed to discipline it. Midway down her back it ran riot. Hardly anything to attract a man. Green eyes that always seemed slightly out of focus. With a start she pulled her spare pair of glasses out of the vanity drawer and put them on. The thin, gamine face became instantly clearer, more dignified. And the bridge of the spectacles covered the line of freckles that were strung out across the base of her nose. Strange how thin her face had become; at eighteen her cheeks had been chubby, and the two dimples popped in at the merest smile!

She pushed the glasses back up her nose with one finger, then brought the finger down across her full red lips, her sharp chin, as she leaned back. A short neck, nothing to boast about there. Clear white skin, and shoulders that sloped slightly, small breasts. Pert, Alfred had said on that mad night, before she'd hit him. A good handful, he had said, and she had hit him again and run!

Good legs, she assured herself as she stood up. Good for running, that is. Slim thighs, swelling hips, a narrow waist. Good lord, here I am going into the most important battle of my life, weaponless!

She made a face at herself. Pull yourself together, Molly Patterson, she ordered. Stop all this mooning, and go downstairs and eat a little supper!

Getting away from the vanity mirror was the most difficult of her many problems. She suddenly felt like an old lady, fumbling to make her legs perform to command. But after that difficulty, the rest was easy. She let her shining hair hang free down her back, and went to check her wardrobe.

As with almost any schoolteacher, her closet was filled with dark slacks and replaceable blouses. Two businesslike dresses, of course, for Parents' Night. One slinky knee-length, just for devilry. One evening gown, in case Sir Lancelot took a wrong turn off Highway 128. Which didn't leave much choice.

With trembling hands she replaced her skirt and blouse with the very slinky dress, and walked slowly down the stairs.

The Hollands were still at the table in the kitchen, holding a family conference—which ceased the moment the door-hinge squeaked and Molly came in. She coughed a couple of times to clear her throat. It was hard to keep the colour from flooding her cheeks.

'I made a mistake in the menu,' she said gruffly. 'The cornflakes were for tomorrow. Tonight we have steak.' She had her back to them as she fumbled in the refrigerator. One quick look in the mirror over the sink showed that they were all smiles, although they said nothing. Neither of them noticed her slinky dress. So much for hunting the male, she told herself disgustedly. She bit her lip as she went on with the work.

Moments later, with the steaks in the broiler, she went back into the refrigerator again for her own meal.

'You're not having steak, Aunt Molly?' Moira had jumped down from the table and came over to her side. 'What's that?'

'Cornish hen,' muttered Molly as she set the little bird in a microwave dish and covered it.

'Cornish hen? I don't understand.'

Molly stopped her preparation and knelt to look the little girl squarely in the eye.

'It's a bird,' she explained slowly. 'It's as close as I can get.'

'To what?' Moira insisted. Her quick-witted father was making choking noises from his place at the table. When he finally managed to swallow and clear his throat he tapped the table a couple of times.

'Don't ask your aunt any more questions,' he managed to gasp. 'Come and sit down, Moira, before Molly burns the steaks!'

The steaks had not burned, although the rock-hen was somewhat underdone. Moira chattered away about school, and by the time the meal was over Molly was feeling just a little more normal. They all helped with the washing up, then decamped to the living-room. Moira already had homework, but it seemed more joke than labour, if one could judge from the giggles emanating from the corner where she was at work.

'And how was *your* day?' Molly asked softly. Tim looked over at her, sitting in her usual deep-cushioned chair, her knitting bag at her side.

'Always busy, Moll?' he replied. 'I remember that well. No matter what was going on, your hands were always busy.'

'And I remember well,' she chuckled, 'how skilful you were at evading questions! How was your day?'

'You're going to catch cold wearing that dress,' he commented.

'Timmy!'

'My day? Somewhere between awful and catastrophic,' he admitted ruefully. 'The freezer plant is working at half capacity, four of our boats are laid up, and there are all sorts of creditors snapping at my—feet.'

Molly coiled her feet up under her in the chair and picked up her needlepoint. Sympathy was one thing he didn't need at the moment, she told herself. 'About par for the course, then?' She gave him a wicked grin, which served to dispel his frown. He leaned back in his chair and winked at her.

'About par for the course,' he agreed. 'There's plenty of material to work with. All I need to do is stave off the creditors with one hand, and push the efficiency button with the other. Easy!'

'Well, I'm glad that's settled.' Her needle clicked as she followed the pattern with half her mind. 'Now we can deal with the important stuff, like Moira has to have some school uniform, and tell me something more about how your aunt Gerda is getting along, and is Captain Francis still aboard the *Ocean Princess*?'

In the lamplight Tim's face was half shadowed, but Molly would have sworn he hesitated and took a deep breath before he answered. 'Yes, of course she has to have school uniform,' he agreed pleasantly. 'So you order it!'

'I did.' It was hard to hide the laugh. Molly turned sideways in her chair to observe more fully. She had him in a corner, and had always loved to watch him try to wriggle out. 'And your aunt?'

'Well—er——' he hedged, 'I think Captain Francis has retired. In fact, so has *Ocean Princess*. We ought to look him up some time, I suppose.'

'Yes, I suppose so.' Molly manufactured an artificial sigh. 'He's such a good man. And he has a nice little house over in the village, on Flume Street, near the church. Now, about Aunt Gerda?'

'Well,' blustered Tim, 'if you knew all that, why were you asking me?' Typical Timmy, she thought. The best defence is a good offence. 'We really should go and visit him—you're right.'

'Best fleet manager in Gloucester,' Molly insisted. 'If *I* owned a fleet that was badly off I'd sure go ask for advice from someone who knows. Now, about Aunt Gerda?'

'I—advice. What a good idea, Molly! Captain Francis—why didn't I think of him! Don't you think it's time for Moira to get to bed?'

'Yes, right after we mention Aunt Gerda,' she

chuckled. 'Come on, Tim. You never *could* fool me with those evasive tactics. So she kept you informed about me during all those years. And then what?'

'Why would you want to know about her?' he demanded truculently.

'Because she's the finest relative you have, and the closest, and I always admired her, and she loves children, so why didn't you go to your aunt with Moira and your problem?'

'I couldn't,' he said solemnly. 'Aunt Gerda is suffering from a terminal disease that's completely incapacitated her. She's totally unable to take care of a little child. Especially a little handicapped child.' He turned his head in Molly's direction, flashed a solemn but soft smile, and looked her straight in the eye—a sure indication that he was lying like a sailor in a foreign port!

'She must have an active ghost.' Molly stabbed her needle into the work in front of her and set it down in her lap. 'She's sent me a birthday card every year, including this one.'

'Birthday——' Tim muttered, then recovered. 'Oh, of course! She arranged for that sort of thing through her lawyer, you know. I get one too. Lovely thought.'

'Lovely,' Molly agreed. 'Her lawyer must be a lovely lady. Her voice on the telephone sounded just like Aunt Gerda. She called me tonight, faker, wanting to know if I had any idea where you were!'

Tim collapsed in his chair, nonplussed. 'My aunt called you?'

'About five o'clock, Timothy. From her home in Framingham.'

'Oh, boy,' he grumbled, shaking his head in disgust. 'Nothing ever goes right, does it? Whom can you trust?'

'She tells me she offered you some—advice—a month ago.'

'Gave me some orders, you mean,' he groaned. 'Knocked me down, turned me inside out, and gave me some instructions.'

'Such as?'

'I—can't tell you that, Moll. It's her secret, and you know I wouldn't betray someone else's secret, would I?'

'No, of course not.' Molly managed another artificial sigh. 'But I suppose I can get it out of her in time. I invited her to come and spend the winter with us. She'll be along next week some time. And *now* I suppose it's time for little girls to hit the sack. Come on, Moira.'

As she walked out of the door she managed to catch one moment when Tim's face was directly in the lamplight. He wore the sombre frown of a boy who had stolen two apples and found them both green.

'You was teasing my dad,' the little girl accused Molly as they went up the stairs hand in hand.

'Guilty, Your Honour,' Molly admitted with a grin. 'I love to do that. Your father sometimes becomes pompous. He fills himself with ideas that he can't share with mere females. Obviously your great-aunt twisted his tail.'

'Did what?'

'Gave him a bad time,' Molly translated. 'Into the tub, love. Cleanliness is next to—I forget what.'

'You do not,' Moira answered solemnly. 'I don't think you ever forgot nothin' at all. Sister Alice said you was the best rememberer in the whole school in all her years of teaching. And that must be a lot, 'cause she taught you when you was a kid, and you're very old now.'

'Wash behind your ears,' her aunt Molly directed in very chilling tones. 'Very old, indeed!'

CHAPTER FOUR

AUNT GERDA arrived on Thanksgiving morning, the last Thursday in November, a national holiday in the United States, where feasting sometimes prevailed over thanks. She came early. Molly and Shag were waiting on the front porch, bundled against the threat of snow. Tim was still in bed; so was Moira.

The little lady, on the shady side of sixty, climbed out of her ancient limousine as if all her bones ached. She was no stranger to Cape Ann. Tim's aunt Gerda had been making this trip three or four times a year for, as she proclaimed, 'A weekend in the country.' Molly had repaid in kind by making an equal number of trips in the other direction each year. She and Gerda Messier were two of a kind, and on a first-name basis.

William, the seventy-year-old chauffeur, remained in his seat as was their custom when the little lady travelled. 'You go for your vacation now, Will,' Aunt Gerda lectured. 'Florida. I left you plenty of money. And put some of that eucalyptus oil on your arm. You hear me?'

'Aye,' the old man replied, even though they all knew he would almost certainly never comply. 'That stuff stinks, Gerda.'

'Stink or not, you put it on, or I'll—oh, good morning, Molly. I have to give Will his orders or he won't take care of himself.'

'Yes,' Molly agreed. 'And I'll just get your luggage while you do.'

The four suitcases in the boot were heavy. Molly,

despite her size, found she could not move their weight, hide her laughter, or sympathise properly as Gerda required with every tenth word. So instead she piled all the cases up just beside the porch step.

'And don't you dare forget to wear your flannels, Will!'

'In Florida?'

'Even in Florida. You have a weak chest.' And with that parting shot Aunt Gerda fluttered away from the car and waved. Will set the car in motion and zoomed away.

'I have such a hard time with Will,' sighed Gerda as she came over to Molly and stood on tiptoe to kiss her cheek. 'He needs managing, you know.'

'Doesn't everyone?' Molly laughed softly as she slipped her arm around her favourite visitor.

'Yes, I think you're right,' Gerda replied as she looked around with an estimating eye. 'Now, let me see what I have to do to get things organised around here!'

By now Molly was looking down at the little lady with a big grin on her face. There was no doubt about it, Aunt Gerda, flighty as a hive of honey bees with no queen, was filled with the compulsion to manage everything and everyone about her. And yet she looked such a gentle soul in her deep blue cloth coat, her little pillbox hat—and yes, even a muff!

'Now where's that good-for-nothing nephew of mine?' the little lady asked.

'Well, I honestly don't know,' said Molly. 'When last I heard, he was snoring away in bed. Come on in, Aunt Gerda, and let's have breakfast, shall we?'

'I didn't get this round by saying no to a good meal,' Aunt Gerda replied, patting herself amidships. 'And then we'll get that man out of bed and he can carry my luggage!'

'That's where I got that idea,' Molly told her. 'Men are meant for carrying things, right?'

'You never said a truer word,' Aunt Gerda replied solemnly. The pair of them marched up the stairs and paraded across to the kitchen. 'But I never expected *him* to move in on you, Molly. Shameful!'

'Oh, I don't mind,' Molly replied gently. 'It seems to me, over the years, that Tim was always moving in on someone!'

'If I'd known, Molly Patterson, I would have been down here like a shot! Imagine the gall of the man, alone in this house with you for weeks! Oh, for breakfast, I'd like something light, of course,' the little lady continued. 'I had toast and tea in Framingham, I do so hate to eat before a trip, especially a long trip. A weak stomach, you know. A family trait.'

'Of course,' Molly agreed, knowing from past experience that the Holland family was equipped with cast-iron stomachs. 'It must be all of twenty-five miles from here to Framingham. How about bacon and eggs, toast, coffee, orange juice?'

'Nice. But where's that great-niece of mine? I've never met the child.'

'You've never met the child?' Molly turned away from the coffee-pot and stared. Tim had hinted that Aunt Gerda knew everything there was to know about Moira. He had also taken evasive tactics when the subject came up again. To be specific, he had almost swallowed his Adam's apple trying to keep her from meeting Aunt Gerda again. Why? Obviously because the dear woman knows something that he doesn't want *me* to know, Molly thought. Which is why I invited her to come and stay with us! Two can play at this game, friend Timothy! And if I get out my shovel and dig deep enough, I'll find out!

Unfortunately for Molly, it was some time later before she found out that there were *more* than two players at the board.

Geared up to peer and pry, she had barely managed to get her mouth open when Moira came strolling into the kitchen, swinging an old tired Raggedy Ann doll by one arm. The little girl was combed and washed and neat, but still in one of the long nightgowns Molly had found for her on one of their many shopping expeditions. 'Look what I found!' the girl chirped.

'My goodness!' said Molly. And then, because in more than a week of hard work the child had mastered more than two hundred words and constructions in American Sign language, she clapped her hands for attention and signed, 'My favourite doll, love. And this is your great-aunt Gerda.'

'May I play with her?' the child signed back. Molly, half of whose mind was on the bacon, was startled into speech.

'Play with Aunt Gerda?'

'No, silly,' Moira laughed, 'with the doll!'

'What's going on here?' A baritone rumble. Tim was at the door, unshaven, hair not brushed, rubbing at his eyes with one knuckle. He looked them all over as if he had stumbled into a bunch of strangers.

Moira giggled. 'I love you,' she signed. Not to be outdone, Molly signed, 'I love you too,' and grinned at him expectantly.

He stretched, touching the top of the door with his upswept hands. 'Well, I can see you've both been studying hard,' he rumbled. 'And I suppose that little bit of fingering means good morning? Show me how you do it.'

'You guessed!' Molly jumped in first, before Moira

could give the right translation, and very solemnly demonstrated to his satisfaction. 'Breakfast?'

'Yeah, I——' he yawned, but Aunt Gerda had outwaited her patience.

'First things first,' she ordered. 'Timothy——' He made a face at the formality of it all. 'Timothy,' his aunt repeated firmly, 'Molly is making my breakfast. And she's making the Thanksgiving dinner too. So I think it only proper that you go outside and bring in my luggage before the snow starts.'

'But——'

'Good morning, Daddy,' his daughter grinned. He looked down at the child, then around the circle of feminine faces.

'Hooked, by God,' he muttered, and stumbled out of the room.

Aunt Gerda stared after him, shaking her head from side to side. 'What that man needs is a shave and a haircut and a good woman to take him in hand,' she said.

'That's true,' Moira commented solemnly.

'I believe you're right,' Molly said under her breath, but two pairs of eyes staring at her announced that they had heard. With a very self-satisfied look on her face Aunt Gerda assaulted her plate of bacon and eggs. Moira pulled up a chair beside her and watched her neat, gentle, but efficient dispatch of the food.

'Are you really my aunt?'

'Only one in existence,' Gerda announced between mouthfuls, and then, dating herself, 'You bet your bippie, kid!'

Molly, feeling a greater warmth in the room than she had first noticed, looked at the two of them carefully inspecting each other, feeling each other out, and smiled. Not just for them, but for herself too. In a place where joy is shared, there are often crumbs of happiness, even for outsiders. And who knows, she asked herself, how many members the Holland family might yet count?

Thanksgiving dinner was typically off schedule. They finally sat down to eat at three in the afternoon, 'Because that leaves more time for snacking later,' Aunt Gerda insisted. Molly, swept up in the tide of being managed, even in her own home, just laughed and agreed. Roast stuffed turkey was, of course, the entrée, done to a turn, surrounded by mashed potatoes, mashed turnips, carrots, peas, green salad, and cranberry sauce. And then three kinds of pie: blueberry, pumpkin, and apple, with real whipped cream. 'An' you have to eat it, Daddy,' Moira insisted. 'I whipped it all by myself!'

'So there's hope for you yet,' he laughed as he ruffled her hair. 'For the longest time I thought you were going to grow up to be a boy!'

'Oh, Daddy!' Accompanied by a long disgusted sigh, such as only a youngster could manage.

But with almost everything eaten, he had the colossal nerve to escape into the living-room with his daughter. 'To play chess,' he announced grandly. Molly sat at table, both elbows on it, looking around at the mass of left-overs, the mountains of dirty dishes, the oceans of pots and pans in the kitchen, and she sighed too. 'At least he might have offered to help with the dishes,' she grumbled.

Aunt Gerda, equally full, shook her head and grinned. 'A man?' she asked cynically. 'Doing dishes on Thanksgiving Day? You expect too much, Molly. Maybe in fifty years or so—but not in my lifetime. Come on, I'll give you a hand.'

Molly came wearily to her feet. In order to stuff and

slow-roast the turkey she had been up at six in the morning. The pies had been made the night before. 'I wonder how they managed on the first Thanksgiving,' she mused.

'Wooden platters,' Gerda suggested. 'Everybody brought something to the feast.'

'Yeah, but the women had to cook it,' Molly chided. 'Aunt Gerda, why did Tim come back home?'

'Why?' Hidden behind a big apron, Aunt Gerda hesitated. 'Because he remembered the girl he left behind?' she asked brightly.

'Oh, come on now. After all that time? I doubt if he even remembered what I looked like. He said he talked to you?'

'Big mouth, he is,' his aunt replied. 'Talks a lot. He's continually running around with shoe-prints on his tongue! Where does this go?'

'Right into the dishwasher,' Molly directed. 'Now, you were saying?'

'I don't believe I was, was I?' the older woman asked vaguely.

'But you were going to,' Molly insisted. She stopped to wipe a drop of water from her eye, and so missed the frantic expression on Aunt Gerda's face, as that lady started out on one of the biggest lies of her life.

'Yes, of course, Molly. Well now.' Gerda pulled out a kitchen chair and sat down. 'Yes. Tim telephoned me as soon as he arrived back in the States. That would be about—oh—three months ago.'

'That long ago?'

'Well, maybe not. You know, I'm not much good with figures.'

'Funny,' Molly mused, 'I somehow had the idea that he was just back from Europe, and came directly—I guess I must have been mistaken. Go on.'

'Well, he explained about Moira's problems and asked my advice, and I remembered your write-up in the papers, about how good you were with deaf kids, so I mentioned your name and he decided to come and—and that's all I know.'

'And about the money, of course?' Molly prodded. Aunt Gerda looked startled, but quickly recovered.

'Oh—yes, of course. About the money. Did you want to freeze the rest of the turkey meat, or leave it out for snacks?'

Even a girl as dumb as I am can recognise that she's slammed the information door shut, Molly sighed to herself. 'Just leave it,' she said. 'It will all get eaten before nightfall, I suppose. Shall we join the others?'

Late that night, with Gerda and Moira both in bed, Molly came back downstairs. Tim was in the living-room, struggling with the sports section of the *Globe*. He looked up when she came in.

'Looks like the Red Sox are headed for last place next year,' he commented. Molly tendered a smile as she swept her skirts under her and sat down opposite him. As with all followers of the New England professional baseball team, it was always 'Wait till next year!' in the hot-stove league. But the Sox were not her major interest.

'I had a long talk with Gerda,' she announced. Tim winced and ducked behind his newspaper. She leaned forward and tugged at the bottom of it until he relented.

'Now,' Molly settled back in her chair, 'Gerda tells me that you asked for her advice about Moira and her problem, and that your aunt referred you to me. How come, Timmy, when we talked, you and I, it didn't come out quite that way?'

'I don't think I understand,' he sighed, setting his paper aside. 'What are you suggesting?'

'You gave me the impression that all this effort was because you'd lost all your money——'

'Well, not all of it,' he interrupted. 'Be fair! I didn't say all of it, Molly.'

She sniffed at him, but her eyes were blinded by that aura that had always affected her whenever she found herself within yards of Tim Holland. 'I suppose you didn't,' she continued firmly. 'But your aunt tells me that you came back from Europe, and you came up here, principally because of Moira's handicap.'

'Just speaking theoretically,' he asked cautiously, 'suppose that were true?'

'Oh, Tim! ' Molly was up out of her chair like a shot, settling in beside him on the couch. 'Don't you really see? You tell me it's all a money problem, when actually it's much more high-principled than that! Knowing that you've put that little girl first—that's important! It gives things a patina of morality that I can appreciate so much better!' It also earned a quick kiss for his cheek, which he in no way tried to avoid.

'Higher morality?' he mumbled. 'Yes, of course. I was——'

'Trying to hide it all behind a macho approach about dirty money,' she interjected. 'I like you better when you take the high road!'

'On the other hand,' he sighed, 'that just might be Molly Patterson, striving to think better about her friends than they deserve. Do you really like Moira?'

'Don't spoil my day,' she lectured. 'Yes, I really like Moira. It's not hard to love her, you know. It's my privilege to have her here—and you too, of course!' She blushed at the omission.

'Thanks for the enthusiasm,' he retorted wryly. 'What is that language you're teaching her?'

'American Sign language,' Molly explained. 'There are two types of sign used in the United Sates. The most popular one is called Signed English. It consists of a series of signs that support the standard English language, vocabulary and syntax. That's what you see on television, when somebody is speaking the words and making signs at the same time. But American Sign is different. It's a complete language with its own grammar, making an integrated whole. A person using Signed English has to know the spoken language beforehand—know it well, and that's hard if you're born deaf to begin with. With ASL you get the whole ball of wax, and can express yourself better.'

'And just how do you know all this?'

'Schools, practice—and more practice,' she teased. 'I'm not the same little girl you left, Tim. Time has passed for me too.'

'I know,' he said seriously, reaching out for one of her hands. 'But it's hard to accept the change. I guess I thought we could come home, you know, and everything could be as it was. Instead—maybe it's better!'

'Why, what a nice thing to say!' she laughed. 'Now *that's* something I'll have trouble getting accustomed to—gallant Timothy!'

'Try it, you'll love it,' he chuckled. He might have said something more, but at that moment Shag blundered into the room. The big dog, moving slowly as was his wont, carefully skirted the coffee-table, sat down in front of Molly, and whined.

'You need to go out?' Molly managed to free herself from Tim's grasp, and stood up. I wonder what else he might have said if we weren't interrupted, she reflected as she patted the dog's head. 'Out?'

Ordinarily Shag would have been at the back door instantly, but not this time. He pawed at her leg and whined again. It was not his regular drill, and Molly was worried. 'Out?' she repeated.

Shag sat back on his haunches and gave an exasperated little bark, then whined again. 'Trouble?' Molly asked. 'Go, Shag.'

It was the right command. The old dog yapped and headed towards the stairs, pausing at the door to be sure she was following. 'Back in a minute,' Molly tossed over her shoulder to Tim, and padded up the stairs behind the animal. The trail led them down the second-floor corridor to the very back of the house, and Moira's room. The door was closed.

Through the thickness of the old walls came the sound of someone crying. Molly grasped the knob of the door and walked into the darkness, Shag hard on her heels. Two strikes on me already, Molly told herself as she fumbled in the dark. No bell-lights, so the child can know someone wants to come in. And no night-lights. For a person with hearing handicaps, the lack of light means the lack of *any* communication.

The sobs were coming from the bed. Molly managed to find the reading lamp on the table beside the big four-poster, and snapped it on. Little Moira was sitting up, her hands clasped around her knees, crying her heart out.

The pain struck at Molly again. This little bundle of child, who had more burdens to bear than most, had completely stolen her heart. She knelt by the bed, crooning softly. The little girl might not have heard, but she toppled to one side in Molly's direction, until she fell straight into the warm arms which were reaching out a welcome.

'Aunt Molly?' Racked with sobs, the words barely came out.

'I'm here,' Molly whispered. 'I'm here.'

'Aunt Molly?' No explanation, no other words. With a sigh the tears came to an end, the little warm body wriggled closer, the little head rested on Molly's shoulder, and Moira went back to sleep.

But five minutes of kneeling in an awkward position put an unusual strain on Molly's back and shoulder. She tried to move to an easier position, but every change brought a whimper from Moira. Finally she gave up. In one quick move she stood up, picked up the warm little body, and settled it and herself down in the middle of the bed. The whimpers trailed off as the child slept. Molly, worn by a long day at hard labour, had intended to rest there only for a moment. Her eyelids were heavy, and when she let them drop, just for a minute, she was unable to recover.

Some twenty minutes later Tim came up the stairs, looking for the comfort and conversation he had expected. Two steps into the room demonstrated to him just how much of an outsider *he* was. Child and woman, they slept together, arms around each other, oblivious to the world.

'Molly?' he whispered tentatively. No answer.

'Molly,' he said softly, 'I wish you could love me as much as you love my daughter.' His face set in stern lines, he went back downstairs to test the quality of the brandy he had brought home from Boston.

CHAPTER FIVE

WINTER seized New England by the throat after Thanksgiving, and shook it until life almost came to a halt. Some eighteen inches of snow fell, in three different storms. By the time the city and the county had dug themselves out there were six-foot drifts along the sides of roads, and piled in odd corners. On the Wednesday before Christmas, the beginning of the school holidays, Molly had put in four hours of hard labour at St Agnes School. Three more partially deaf students had enrolled, and the entire school body was clamouring for sign-language instruction.

'I don't mind, if you think it will do some good,' Molly told Sister Alice.

'It's doing a great deal of good,' the Principal replied. 'Not only are they learning something practical, but they're also becoming more sensitive about other people's problems. I approve, Father Mulcahey approves——'

'And the Bishop?' Molly teased.

'And the Bishop *would* approve if someone ever told him about it,' Sister Alice said primly. 'Now, how can you go about it?'

'Very simply,' Molly explained. 'We'll use the old Mexican system, called Each one Teach one. I'll present classes to some of the seniors, they in turn will scatter, and each one will teach one of the other students.'

So for the first three weeks of December the scheme was applied. It raised the very devil with schedules, but none of the other teachers complained—in fact, most of them were learning for themselves. And then, on the Wednesday half-day, things had ground to a halt for the ten-day holidays.

'We're lucky,' said Moira cheerfully as she and Molly waded through the drifts and piled into the Bronco.

'Of course we are,' Molly agreed as she stepped into one drift deeper than her boots were high. 'Why?'

'Why? Well, because——' Moira laughed. 'Because we have four-wheel drive, among other things. And because it's Christmas—and because I'm famous! Oh, Aunt Molly!' She threw herself across the bench seat and wrapped her arms around her adopted aunt. Startled, Molly looked down. There were two tiny tears in the child's eyes.

'Crying?' She peeled off her thick mitten and pulled back the hood of the girl's heavy coat. 'Tears?'

'Happy tears,' Moira explained, wiping them away with the sleeve of her coat. 'Happy tears. I don't remember ever bein' so happy waiting for Christmas to come. And it's all your fault, Aunt Molly!'

'You're so happy you're crying, and it's all my fault?'

'So maybe I don't got—maybe I don't have the right words,' Moira sniffled. 'I didn't mean it was your *fault*, exactly. I meant you were the cause of it all, like. I mean——'

'I know,' Molly laughed. 'Don't try to explain it any further; ideas like that tend to get caught up in a mess. Leave it. But I *am* intrigued by the other part. You're famous?'

Moira flashed her patented wide-angle grin. 'I'm famous,' she averred. 'All over the school, everybody knows me—an' likes me, Aunt Molly. Would you believe that? I never knew so many kids before, and they all like me! I used to think that if a kid had one friend she was doing OK, you know, but there's hundreds of kids in that school——' the little girl paused to take a deep breath. '—and every one of them likes me!'

Molly started the engine, and waited for it to warm up before commenting. 'I think that's wonderful,' she said. 'You must have worked hard to gain their trust and all——'

Moira laughed. 'Me?' she gasped as she caught her breath. 'Not me! I'm famous because you're my aunt Molly! You're the one who's teaching lip-reading and sign language, and they like that, especially because to fit that in Sister Alice has had to cut down the spelling and the music classes!'

'Oh, me!' groaned Molly as she shifted into gear and started down Pleasant Street. 'You're famous because I've cut in on spelling!'

'Don't knock it,' the child said. 'You adults wouldn't really know about spelling and such.'

'Hey,' Molly objected as she swung the car down towards the docks. 'I was a kid once myself, you know. And in this very same school!' For the next few minutes she concentrated on her driving, but out of the corner of her eye she could see Moira solemnly shaking her head from side to side, as if denying that any present-day adult could ever really have been a child! But there was one thing very apparent. In the course of the last few weeks Moira had gradually lost some of her reserve—some of that shyness that followed handicapped children through their days.

Out of habit Molly drove down around the Harbour loop, then along the shore to the docks where the Holland Ocean Fisheries warehouses stood. As usual at the beginning of the Christmas season, most of the fleet was tied up. All eight boats of the Holland company were—eight? Molly brought the Bronco to a slipshod stop and counted again. Eight boats, thirty to fifty feet long, their decks covered with snow, their rigging a solid mass of ice. And only three weeks ago there had only been four Holland boats.

And there, coming along the sidewalk in his fisherman's rolling walk, was Captain Francis! Molly leaned across Moira and rolled the window down.

'Captain Ahab!' she called. Another local joke, calling the elderly captain by the name of the ship captain in the novel *Moby Dick*. He recognised her, made his way to the side of the car, and leaned in the open window. 'Well, I do declare,' the old man chuckled. 'Nobody's called me Ahab since——'

'I'm sorry,' Molly apologised. 'It's just an old bad habit. Have you met Moira Holland?'

'Ah!' One of his giant arms came through the window, and a rough sea-reddened hand swallowed up Moira's little paw. 'Tim's girl, hey?' After many years at sea, the Captain's conversational voice was just a little short of hurricane force. Moira nervously moved closer to Molly, but she said not a word as her hand was vigorously massaged.

'Yup,' the old man continued, 'ain't nobody called me Ahab since I took over the direction of the whole Holland fleet. Smart young man, your father, little miss.'

'You're scaring her half to death,' Molly told him. 'Took over the entire fleet, did you? When was that?'

'Ayup. About a month 'fore Thanksgiving, it were. Got me a call from Washington, from that young whippersnapper Tim Holland. Git your—oops, I can't say them words. Get yourself in gear, he sez to me, right on the telephone, and git over to the boats. I want to know how come we got more crew than fish! Mighty forceful, that man of yours, Miss Molly!'

A month before Thanksgiving? Long before I suggested the idea, he'd already taken steps. Suddenly deflated, Molly said defensively, 'He's not *my man*. But I'm glad you got the job. Couldn't happen to a smarter man!'

'Ayup.'

Doing her best not to giggle, Molly worked around to what she really wanted to know. 'So how come you have so many boats now?'

'Oh, them?' He waved a casual hand towards the fishing craft, tied up alongside each other. 'Ain't the half of it,' he chuckled. 'The *Barbara Anne*'s over on the other side. Just unloaded forty-three thousand pounds of mixed. And the *Theresa Marie*'s standing by to unload. They got about forty thousand pounds aboard!'

'But—I thought the company was——'

'Ain't never been in better shape,' Captain Francis chuckled. 'That Tim, he's about as sharp as his grandpa was, and tough as a nail. They don't make them kind no more!'

'No, they don't,' Molly commented as she rolled the window up and started off again. No, they don't. It's almost impossible to find a man with such a slippery tongue as Tim Holland's. The money's gone. Hah! Bankruptcy stares us in the face! Yeah! And we've put four more boats to sea, at least. Four boats!

'What did you say?' Moira was looking up at her, curiosity written in every pore.

'Nothing.' Molly shrugged. 'Starting to snow again. What say, shall we dash for home, or find a restaurant and have some lunch?'

'I vote for the restaurant,' Moira squealed. 'Then I

won't have to do the dishes!'

'What a lovely sentiment!' Molly chided. 'And instead we leave Aunt Gerda all alone in the house!'

'Only for a little while,' begged Moira. Molly found it impossible to avoid that lovely begging little face.

'All right,' she agreed. 'I'll call her from the restaurant.'

The car skidded as they turned back to East Main Street. In typical Yankee fashion there was no West Main Street. Instead, at the five points where East Main, Commercial, Rogers, and Washington Streets met up, the artery going westward was known as Western Avenue, a suitable compromise.

Because of the snow and the threat of more, half of Main Street was closed, but the sign on the Down-East Restaurant and its associated Oyster Bar was still lit. Molly managed to squeeze her car into a parking space someone else had shovelled—a terrible crime in Massachusetts—and hurried Moira inside. The sudden warmth, the homey atmosphere, struck them like a solid blow. They struggled out of their winter gear, then followed the manager to an empty table in the far corner.

'Now you see what you want to order,' Molly dictated, 'while I go and make that call to Aunt Gerda.'

'I *know* what I want,' Moira replied. But Molly was halfway across the room, heading for the telephone booths. There was some difficulty with the lines. Molly remembered driving north from Magnolia barely five hours earlier, and seeing the cables alongside the road bowing under the weight of snow and ice. Eventually, with the help of an operator, she made the contact.

'Don't worry about me' Aunt Gerda responded cheerfully. 'I've got my novel, and the house is nice and warm, and Shag is here to look after me. So you both stay and have a good time.'

All of which sent Molly back to the table in good spirits, only to find that the child had accumulated a pair of adult companions. The room was not brightly lit, and her glasses were fogged over, so it was not until she reached the table that Molly recognised Tim, carrying on a casual conversation with his daughter. He rose to greet Molly, and held her chair.

'This *is* a surprise,' he commented as he sat down between Molly and Moira. 'I thought surely the weather would keep you both home.'

'Not a chance,' his daughter said in a very subdued voice. 'There's always school, you know. And Aunt Molly is the best teacher there is!'

'Why, of course she is,' said the little woman sitting on Molly's other side. 'Always dependable Molly. Hello, Moll.'

By that time Molly had managed to get her eyes focused and her glasses off the ridge of her nose. Which was probably the best thing she could do as she stared—and felt her world fall into little pieces, like the snow melting off her coat collar. Her worst fear had come true.

'Hello, Susan,' she answered bleakly, and turned to stare at Tim with a haunted expression in her eyes.

'Susan and I have a family problem to work out,' Tim said cautiously.

'That's nice,' Molly said vaguely. 'That's nice. I——'

'Why, I haven't seen you since my wedding day,' Susan offered. There was all the comfort of a cobra about to strike, wrapped in her sharp soprano voice. 'Moira, did you know that Molly was my bridesmaid?' She might just as well have reached over and stabbed Molly in the back. And the little girl was not too comfortable either. She shifted and rocked in her chair for a moment, and then tried unobtrusively to slide it farther in her father's direction.

'Moira, your mother is talking to you,' Tim prodded gently. The child flared up.

'I don't have any mother,' the child snapped. 'I only got Aunt Molly!'

'That's enough of that,' her father reprimanded. 'Now, what would you two like for lunch?'

'I ain't hungry,' Moira said stubbornly, and looked an appeal across the table towards Molly.

'Come to think of it, I'm not hungry either,' Molly asserted. 'And it's beginning to snow very hard, and Aunt Gerda is all alone in the house, and I think we'd better——'

Tim's big hand caught her as she pushed her chair back. 'I know you're a lot of crazy things, but I've never known you to be a coward, Molly,' he said in an undertone. She shook her hand free.

'Then you haven't known me as well as you thought,' she muttered. 'I'm not going to sit here and—well, I'm not.' And then, in a tone of exaggerated deference, 'Would you wish your daughter to stay with you, or shall I take her along?'

'Oh, God,' Tim moaned. 'Why me, God?'

'So we'll have that cosy tête-à-tête after all,' Susan interrupted. 'But I did want to talk to my daughter, Timothy, love.'

'I'm gonna go with Molly,' said Moira, shoving her chair back abruptly. 'Why did you have to come and spoil everything?'

'Moira!' Tim commanded.

'Well, really, this doesn't boost your case at all!' snapped Susan. 'Such disgusting manners! She didn't behave like that in *my* care.'

'I don't think she could, seeing that you abandoned her before she could talk,' Tim said bitterly.

'Now, now, Timmy, we mustn't make nasty statements like that. Especially since *we* want something from Susan so very badly,' Susan retorted. 'I've changed my mind. Run along, Moira. Run along with your aunt Molly. And Molly, you really must do something with that hair. Even spinsters have to have some minimum care about their looks! Nothing to say?'

'Nothing,' seethed Molly. 'Nothing at all. Drink your coffee. It'll be good for you.' She stalked out of the room, struggling with her coat and scarf, with Moira close behind her.

The wind howled down the street, driving snowflakes in front of it. The car was cold, and gave trouble starting. Molly was cold, deep down inside her, where she stored all the cherished things of her life. Not a crowded place, but an important one. Susan back, she told herself as she waited for the motor to warm up. Susan back, and Tim has her. Even my life is back to re-runs. I might as well become a TV soap opera: *The Ten Loves of Molly Patterson.* Isn't it strange that they're all with the same man, and have the same ending? Is God trying to tell me something?

'Couldn't we go?' Moira interrupted. 'I'm cold!'

The trip along Western Avenue was nerve-racking. The roads had been ploughed twice in the last four days, but the falling snow was accumulating again, faster than the local Department of Public Works could move it. The Bronco, with its four-wheel drive engaged, held the crown of the road fairly well, and only an occasional vehicle coming in the other direction forced them off to one side. Magnolia looked like a winter postcard, with nothing stirring, as they switched to Hesperus Avenue and rumbled through the centre of the village and out the other side.

But the wandering road on the other side of Kettle Cove was a different matter entirely. Serving as it did only six or seven houses, it had received only one visit from the snow-ploughs. Their little car bucked and swerved and jumped, and for a time it looked as if they would never make it over the wooden bridge that spanned Colkers Creek, but they did.

'I've never seen anything so beautiful,' Moira commented as they pulled to a stop.

'Anything what?' Molly searched the area, and found nothing particular to note.

'I can't hear you so good.' Moira twisted around in her seat and stared directly at her. 'When I'm like in a car, or someplace where there's noise, my hearing aid picks up all the noises at once, and they sort of drown each other out.'

'That's ridiculous,' said Molly. 'There are half a dozen designs that filter out crowd noises. Expensive, but if your dad is running ten boats, he can afford them.'

'Well, don't get mad at me,' the child said in an injured tone. 'It's not my fault!'

'No indeed, it's not your fault, Moira. Now, what was the something that seemed so beautiful?'

'The house, silly. For the last two miles I was sure we were going to end up in a ditch. Even if the roof blows off, the house looks wonderful!'

'Oh, ye of little faith,' Molly laughed. 'Get in the house, kid!'

Shag met them at the door, followed at length by a startled Aunt Gerda, with a fried chicken leg in her hand. 'I thought you weren't coming,' the elderly lady said questioningly. She waved her chicken leg around like a conductor in the middle of *Messiah*.

'Well, we changed our minds,' Molly reported glumly. 'It was a——'

'They had something on the menu that we couldn't stomach,' Moira interrupted. 'Both of us. I mean, neither of us.'

'Whatever,' Molly concluded for her. 'Any more of that chicken left?'

'Comes frozen, in a package,' Aunt Gerda reported. 'All you have to do is slide a piece or two in the microwave. What do you think?' She waved vaguely in the direction of the Great Outdoors.

'I think we're working up to a blizzard,' said Molly. 'Have you been listening to the radio?'

'Funny you should ask.' Gerda led the way into the warm kitchen. 'Station WEEI claims a nor'easter is building up. They're predicting twelve to twenty inches of snow on top of what we already have.'

'What's that mean—a nor'easter?' Moira demanded to know.

'Just a big storm,' Molly explained. 'One that blows in out of the north-east, and has plenty of moisture picked up from the ocean. The worst kind of storm along these shores. And if their prediction is right, we could be snowed in.'

'Lucky that we stocked up the pantry yesterday,' Aunt Gerda said. 'Isn't there something else we——?'

'Several somethings,' Molly agreed morosely. 'Gerda, you check out the emergency lanterns and candles. Moira, you hop up to the bathroom and fill the tub with cold water—as high as you can, love. And I'll go around the house and get the shutters closed. We may have trouble with the electricity, and we could possibly have a problem with the wind. Scoot, Moira!'

The little girl ran off gleefully, glad to have something to do. Shag meandered along behind her, barely making the stairs. 'So now,' Aunt Gerda said quietly, 'the child is out of the way. What happened?'

Molly shrugged her shoulders. 'Something that's just par for the course for me,' she sighed. 'Every time I locate the tracks that the gravy train runs on, somebody cancels the schedule. We stopped in at the Down East Restaurant, and Tim walked in—you wouldn't believe.'

'I'd believe,' his aunt said grimly. 'I'd believe almost anything about that idiot nephew of mine. He was with someone?'

'He was with his wife,' Molly reported dolefully. 'Susan's back.'

'Oh, my God!'

'My thoughts exactly,' said Molly. 'You wouldn't believe how many fairy-tales I've been dreaming the past few weeks. I thought that pair were divorced!'

'Well, if it's any help to you, they are. You'd better get the shutters, Molly Patterson.'

By three o'clock that afternoon the old Patterson house was battened down, ready for almost anything. Almost, that was the word Molly used to herself, when the big yellow DPW snowplough made an unexpected visit, swiped a circle in front of the house, stopped long enough to let two figures out into the drifts, then ploughed its way back down to Route 127.

'Now what?' Moira came to the door and joined Molly, trying to peer out into the blowing snow. 'I can't believe any sane person would come calling at this hour of the day!'

'No, I guess you're right,' said Molly in stiff unbelief.

'It's your father. And he has someone with him!'

'I don't want to know,' the little girl groaned. 'Shag and I, we're going to go hide in your room, Aunt Molly. Please?' The appealing look again, wistful, begging. Almost Molly agreed, but then had second thoughts.

'Not in *my* room, young lady,' she admonished. 'I've got your Christmas present hidden in my room. If you *have* to be a coward, you——'

'Who's the coward?' Aunt Gerda came up behind them. The figures outside had united somehow or another, and were struggling up the steps to the porch, arm in arm, carrying a couple of suitcases.

'Nobody,' Moira answered glumly. Gerda moved to the door and swung it open. A blast of arctic air, smothered by more than a few snowflakes, flooded the living-room. Propelled by the wind, the pair stumbled in through the door, and it was immediately slammed shut behind them.

'Good lord!' Tim gasped. 'I haven't seen anything like this since the blizzard of '68!' He turned his companion around and began to brush the snow off her coat, and out of her hair. As she revolved under his caring hand, Susan giggled.

'Why, hello, Auntie Gerda,' she trilled. 'I haven't seen you in years! Do you remember me? Susan?'

'I should be so lucky,' muttered Gerda, and then more forcefully, 'Wipe your feet!'

'Well,' the little soprano voice said gleefully, 'not a thing's changed, Tim. Not a thing! And what a warm welcome. Tell them about us!'

Tim had shaken himself down, and was out of his heavy overcoat. 'It's Molly's house,' he said. 'We ask, not tell.'

'Oh, of course. Pardon me.' Divested of her outerwear, Susan was encased in a form-fitting scarlet cat-suit. She twirled around to give them all a good look. Tim's eyes seemed to follow the woman's every movement, Molly noted fiercely. Sickening, she told herself, as she struggled to maintain an outward calm. Sickening. Acts like a twelve-year-old, and wonders why people get angry. Listen to her gush! And why in the name of everything that's holy does she have to be so overwhelmingly beautiful!

Gerda directed Moira in the collection of coats and boots and scarves, while Tim brushed back his hair nervously and came over to where Molly waited, like some frozen statue.

'Susan just came in from Boston a couple of hours ago,' he explained. 'There doesn't seem to be any motel space available. Some sort of mini-convention is going on at the Marina Motor Inn, and all the rest of the motels seem to have accumulated stranded honeymooners and travelling salesmen. So I said to myself——'

'So you said to yourself, why not take her along to good old Molly's place,' Molly interrupted, forcing her voice to sound hospitable. 'And why not, Tim? Any friend of yours is a friend of mine, right?' She waved her finger in front of his nose, the finger with the scar from so long ago.

'Just so.' He broke out his number one grin, from ear to ear. 'So I said to Susan, I'm sure Molly would be happy to put you up for a few days—at least until after the Christmas season.'

Molly, who had never been very good at maths, did a quick study. Two days until Christmas, and then the twelve days to follow? Fourteen days? Two weeks? What was it her very Catholic mother used to say? *Sometimes God acts like a Protestant*! How can I stand it for that length of time? she thought.

But her New England conscience was not about to let her get away with such gibberish. Susan Holland is a guest in your house. It's the season to be merry! And stop moaning and groaning, Molly Patterson. Just because you came in second in the two-woman race for Tim Holland, it doesn't mean you can spend the rest of your life mooning around!

'Yes, of course,' she sighed. 'Of course, she's welcome for as long as she cares to stay. Come along into the kitchen, you two. It's warmer there, and we can have a cup of hot coffee——'

'Tea,' Susan insisted.

'——yes, tea,' Molly amended her statement. *What the devil was that stuff they poured in Socrates' cup*? She shook her head and led the way out into the other room, where Aunt Gerda, who only *looked* like a flighty woman, had made all the arrangements.

The wind seemed to be whistling louder and stronger around the house as they huddled around the kitchen table and watched while Gerda poured the coffee and tea from the same kettle spout. Instant miracles, with instant coffee and now instant tea as well. Susan made a face as she sipped at her mug, but evidently thought better of complaining when she saw Tim staring her down.

'I think we need a council of war,' he commented as he grounded his mug. 'We're in a pretty exposed situation up here on the bluff. What does the weatherman have to say?'

'Before our television antenna blew away, the Channel Four man predicted that the storm could last through the night and perhaps well into tomorrow,' said Gerda.

'And from the looks of things as we drove down from Gloucester,' Molly added, 'we're likely to be snowed in for three or four days.'

'Right through Christmas,' grumbled Moira, feeling sorry for herself.

'How else is St Nicholas going to get here?' her father teased.

'Phoo, who believes in *that*?' The child scraped back her chair and stomped over to the window. At barely four in the afternoon it was already dark outside.

'I'm glad to hear nobody believes,' Aunt Gerda chuckled. 'I can take the presents I bought back to Framingham when I go home.'

'I believe,' Tim said quietly. His daughter stared at him from the window seat, sniffed back a couple of tears, and ran from the room.

'Another display of bad manners,' Susan pointed out maliciously. 'There's no doubt about it, Tim, you haven't done a very good job of raising my daughter.'

He stared at her thoughtfully, as if carefully choosing his words. 'You shouldn't complain, Susan. You can't afford to.'

Whatever the words meant to the others, they struck Susan close to her heart. If she has one, Molly thought. The original ice-maiden!

'How about going on with our inventory?' said Tim. 'How are we fixed for food?'

'Plenty,' Molly reported. 'Perhaps not too fancy, but plenty. If everyone helps out in the kitchen we'll do well.'

'I'm afraid that's something beyond me,' Susan said. 'You'll have to do without me.'

'We can't all be gourmet cooks,' Tim informed her gently. 'So I guess that leaves you with the dishes. Moira can help. What else, Molly?'

'Water,' she said immediately. 'We don't have city water. Everything comes from our well, and the pump is electrical.'

'So then our problem is the electric lines,' Tim mused. 'Didn't you have an emergency power plant?'

'In the barn, Tim,' Molly reported. 'But I haven't used it in a hatful of years. I don't really know if it will start. There's plenty of fuel, but——'

'OK, that will be the first thing for us to look at,' he replied. 'In the meantime, no baths, no showers, minimum water-use starting at once.'

'Oh, no!' Susan stood up so quickly that her chair fell over backwards. 'I can't put up with that!'

'There are lots of things you can put up with if you have to,' Tim growled. 'And now you have to. Anything else, Molly?' He might have considered the subject closed, but Susan certainly did not. With a muffled moan she ran out of the kitchen and up the stairs. Molly moved as if to go after her, but Tim put up a warning hand.

'She—doesn't know the house very well,' Molly protested. 'It's been a pile of years since she's been here.'

'She'll survive. Now, what else?' This is the old Tim, Molly thought. Straight to the point, forceful—male! Where did that idea come from?

'Molly?'

Caught thinking when she should have been listening, she ducked her head to hide her give-away eyes, and fumbled. 'I—think the house has no defects,' she stammered. 'All the shutters are closed. In over two hundred years an Atlantic storm has yet to blow us down. We have plenty of lanterns and candles, if need be, but we must be careful of fire. There's no way the Fire Department could get out here to help. No way. I have an old CB radio someplace or other. I suppose we might rig that up just in case the phone line goes dead. No, I guess that's all, Tim. I'll get out all the stored blankets and sheets, and see everyone gets comfortable.' For everyone read Susan Holland, and I don't care if she's ever comfortable again. And don't tell me, God—I know that's not the Christian way!

'I'd better get moving,' she said. 'I didn't expect Susan. I suppose we——' Her faced turned brick red as she came to an abrupt halt. 'I—suppose she'll—be sharing a room, Tim?'

'I don't know why you'd suppose that,' he laughed, 'unless you mean to take her in with you?' Unable to find the right words, Molly crimsoned again, and strode purposefully for the stairs.

'Now that was mean,' Aunt Gerda lectured him. 'Just plain mean. What are you up to, young man?'

'The same thing I was up to a week ago,' he muttered. 'And don't tell me you don't understand, you scheming old witch.'

'And what kind of way is that for you to talk to your aunt?' Gerda asked cautiously. 'No, wait, don't answer that question. There are a number of things going on in this house, and I'm sure I'd sleep better tonight if I didn't know what they were. But why Susan?'

'I know,' he sighed, scraping at the side of his face with one finger. 'She wasn't in the cards, not by any means. Would you believe I haven't seen her in years? She just popped out of the woodwork today.'

'I believe you,' his aunt said grimly. 'Many wouldn't, but when I was a young girl I used to practise—you know, thinking up one absolutely unbelievable subject every week, and convincing myself it was true!'

'Aunt Gerda!'

'Don't turn up your nose at me, Tim Holland. I know you from a long way back. How do you suppose Molly is going to believe that story? And what exactly does Susan want?'

'For the first question, Susan seems to think she's found a loophole in my divorce settlement. She seems to think she can prove I'm an unsuitable parent, and custody of the child should be given to her,' he sighed.

'And do you think she has a chance of proving that?'

'Who knows, these days?' He shrugged. 'Besides, I think that's only her *stated* goal. What she's really after is a cash settlement. Somehow she's heard that Holland Ocean Fisheries is far from being on its last legs. She wants a bigger cut!'

'And what about what Molly thinks?' His aunt glared at him, demanding an answer he didn't want to give.

'I thought it would all be so easy,' he sighed. 'You know, I'd *seen the light*, so how could it be possible that Molly wouldn't have, too? We were just made for each other, Molly and I. But the way things are going on around here, she's become the relentless best friend, and doesn't mean to stir one centimetre off centre! Whatever happened to *absence makes the heart grow fonder*?'

'Well, I did warn you,' his aunt mused. 'More than once I warned you that you were putting things off to the point of danger!'

'Dammit, you know I couldn't come,' he grumbled. 'There was always that one last chance, just over the hill, that one of those famous European surgeons might be able to cure Moira's problems. I *couldn't* come—not until I got the last negative report.'

'You should have come,' Gerda insisted gently. 'Molly is the kind of woman who would have understood. Or you could have written—or even telephoned.'

'Yeah, sure.' It was a nervous affliction, this running his hands through his hair as he frowned. 'Yeah, sure. What would I have said? Hello, Molly, I'm sorry I picked the wrong woman, but would you mind if I came back and married you?'

'A little abrupt, perhaps,' his aunt commented. 'But it would certainly have been better than this brouhaha that you've thought up. She was down at the docks this morning, counting all the Holland boats, you know. Want to try again about that poverty-stricken act?'

'Oh, God!' he muttered.

'Yes, well, maybe He could help if you asked.' Aunt Gerda, who knew that Tim had not seen the inside of a church since his wedding day, threw in the barbed comment just to see him squirm. After all, she thought, it's all bound to come out right in the end, and in the meantime, nephew or not, he deserved to suffer.

'So you think Susan will involve you in a custody battle?' she repeated.

'I don't really know,' he replied. 'More money, I suppose, might settle the deal. On the other hand, blackmailers never stop. If I gave her money this year she'd probably want more next year, and I'm not about to let her leech on to me like that! On the other hand,' he said worriedly, 'I can't afford to take a chance, can I? Moira's too precious to me for that.'

Gerda's eyes lit up for battle. 'There's no chance of that, Timmy. Even the dumbest judge in the state, and lord knows there are a lot of them, couldn't rule against you. You think she means it?'

'I don't know.' He slammed his fist down on the table for emphasis. 'I don't think so. I think the game is to get me on edge, and try to use Moira as a hostage—something like that. If I could get Molly on my side, there's no court in the world would rule against me. Only I don't understand where Molly's coming from. Is there some other man hiding in the woodwork?'

Gerda leaned back in her chair and nibbled at her lip.

'Well,' she drawled, 'there *was* a name she mentioned a few months ago—in the middle of the summer when she came down to Framingham to visit. Now what was that ridiculous name? Alfred, that's it. Alfred DeMoins.'

'Alfred?' Tim half-closed his eyes as he ran the name through his mental computer. 'Alfred DeMoins? I've heard that name before, but I can't remember where! What are you grinning at?'

'Walter Scott,' his aunt said, and her grin spread all the way across her face. Tim sat up straight and watched his only dear relative, his co-schemer, looking at him like a cat watching a saucer of milk cool.

'Well, don't leave me hanging in mid-air,' he rasped.

'No, of course not.' Gerda, stretching upward to the full limit of her very tiny frame, seemed to overawe him. 'Walter Scott,' she repeated meaningfully. He shrugged defeat. 'Oh what a tangled web we weave, when first we practise to deceive!'

What with one thing and another, Tim knew he would sleep poorly that night. There were half a dozen pills left in his bottle, the palliative for a small accident he had suffered months before. Shrugging his shoulders, he swallowed one, gave life a considered thought, and had another on top of the first.

CHAPTER SIX

IT WAS a night of storm and bluster. The old house creaked and groaned as the wind buffeted it from all sides and whistled at the double chimneys. Molly huddled deep in her bed, her electric blanket no proof against a power failure. She was unable to sleep. Her mind worried at her problem, like a dog worrying a bone. What to do? Tell Tim that she loved him? Don't tell him, and suffer as he played with Susan? And what about Moira? The child needed a woman in her life, but was that sufficient reason to marry Tim? And what about her? Could she survive, needing Tim and not having him; or needing Moira and not having her? Love is a complicated passage, and Molly Patterson had hardly the experience to solve the puzzle.

But Tim was—not exactly the boy she had grown up with. A little too slippery for a country girl to hang on to, a little too ambitious, a little too—free with the truth? There were tears on her pillow and her mind was as untidy as an unmade bed, when the winds came to a sudden halt along about midnight.

The stillness was almost as bad as the storm sounds had been. The house settled down. Feet pattered up and down the hall outside her room. Doors closed surreptitiously. Distressed by her thoughts, Molly pulled herself up in bed and sat there, listening. There were strange additions to all the night noises she remembered. Her Christmas gift to Moira lay in a little basket under her bed and whined. Shag, outside in the corridor, scratched at her door, his nose telling him what his mistress would not.

Like a spider in my web, Molly thought. Tim's room on my right hand, Susan on my left, Moira across the hall, and Gerda at the other end of the corridor. Shag whined again; the little bundle under her bed whimpered, and faintly, from across the hall, Moira started muttering in her sleep.

Molly slipped out of bed, snatched up her warm winter robe and slippers, and made for the door. As soon as the knob turned Shag threw his considerable weight against the panel and forced his way in. 'Well, thank you very much,' Molly whispered sarcastically, but the big dog went straight for his objective. Moira was rambling again.

Stopping just long enough to make sure Shag was not about to create an international incident, Molly padded across the hall and into the little girl's room. The night-light showed the child tossing and turning in her bed. Molly sat down on the edge of the mattress and ran a hand through the girl's lovely hair. 'Easy now,' she crooned, 'Aunt Molly's here.'

One of those beautiful eyes opened, and then the other. 'I don't want you,' the girl muttered. 'I want my dad. I can't trust nobody else! Go away!'

'I couldn't sleep either,' Molly sighed. 'It must be the atmospheric pressure, or something.' The child sat up, resting her head against Molly's breast.

'It was gonna be a wonderful Christmas,' she sighed. 'Why did *she* have to come?'

'She?'

'You know who. Susan!'

'She's your mother, sweetheart. People always love their mothers.'

'No, they don't,' the little rebel said firmly. 'And she's not my mother. She gave up the job a long time ago. I hate her! I thought——' Tears interrupted, and refused to be stanched.

'I want my dad. I want my dad!' The appeal caught at Molly's heart, but there was no solace she could offer. So much bitterness caught up in such a tiny body! So much anger.

'All right,' she said. 'Lie down here. I'll go and call your dad.'

Luckily, at just that moment, Shag wandered into the room behind them. The little girl wanted Molly to go, but refused to release her. Molly urged the big old dog up to the bed where, because of his size, he could lay his muzzle on top of the covers without straining. For a moment the child hesitated then transferred her hold. Shag endured it all patiently.

With knees almost as stiff and strained as her heart, Molly managed to get up. The pair of them, the dog and the girl, remained unmoved. From the doorway Molly looked back. Poor kid, she thought. She can't trust anybody—not yet. Anybody except her father and my dog. For just one bleak second Molly felt the pain at being shut out. She wheeled and went out into the hall on her errand.

Tim's door was shut, but it opened quietly. The room was in total darkness. He had pulled the heavy curtains, and there were no lights left on. Careful to avoid stubbing her toe on something, Molly felt her way across the room in the general direction of the bed. 'Tim?' she whispered. She could hear him breathing heavily. 'Tim?'

There was no change in his breathing. Holding both hands out in front of her as a warning device, Molly continued her wandering. The breathing was coming closer. So was the bed.

Her knees struck the bed-rail before her hands found

any opposition. Although she had been moving slowly she wavered back and forth for a second, lost her balance, and sprawled across the mattress, hands outstretched, landing flat out on top of Tim. 'Oh, God!' she groaned.

He might have been a heavy sleeper, but he had instantaneous male reactions. Both his arms came up and grabbed at her, holding her struggling form down against his naked chest. 'Oh, God,' she muttered again. 'Tim?'

No answer. Instead he rolled over, taking her with him, until they were lying side by side, nose to nose, his hands in total possession. Fight? she asked herself. Scream? Reason with him? Forget it and just lie there in the warmth? Her body was willing, but her Puritan mind rebelled. 'Tim,' she whispered as she struggled to get one hand free. 'Tim!'

'I hate women who come to bed to talk,' he murmured drowsily into her free ear.

'Damn you, Tim Holland,' she whispered. It was terribly hard to conduct a screaming operation when there was a need for silence. 'Tim Holland, turn me loose!' She might have said more, but he closed her mouth effectively by sealing it up with his own lips.

Stunned, Molly relaxed for just that fatal moment that allowed him to penetrate her mouth. And from that point on, it was 'Kate bar the door.' Staid, pragmatic Molly Patterson disappeared in a cloud of dust, to be replaced by a squirming, moaning minx who could just not get close enough. His hands went sensuously down her back, stirring every passion, arousing every nerve-ending. And when he rolled her over, flat on her back, and one of his practised hands easily found the combination to both robe and nightgown, all her tactile senses exploded. His fingers found the stiffened bronze tip of her breast, his mouth teased at her earlobes, then shifted lower. Molly gave up thinking. It seemed the appropriate thing to do. Someone was murmuring in the night, 'Tim, Tim, Tim!' Luckily that's not me, the tiny segment of her brain still in action reported. But of course it was. And it was only that tiny conduit of thought that allowed her to hear Moira's sobs, and remember. With a gigantic effort she tore herself free, rolled again to her right, and landed with her knees on the floor, her nose pressed up against his.

'Tim,' she hissed, 'it's Molly, not Susan!'

'I know who it is,' he answered. 'I never go to bed with strangers, Molly.'

'Oh! You—monster!' she screamed, then clapped her hand over her mouth. 'You—you——!' It was impossible to find the right words. She bolted towards the door, and out into the hall. In the pale light of the hall windows Susan was standing at her own half-opened door, grinning.

'Sweet innocent Molly?' she laughed. 'Bed-hopping, Molly? Won't that look nice in court?' Susan was still laughing as she went back into her room. Molly, shaking, gathered her robe around her and hurried back to Moira's room. The bed was empty. But across the hall, from Molly's own bedroom, there was a little squeal of delight. She followed the sound.

Moira and Shag had transferred from one room to the other, but in the doing the little girl had knocked over the wicker basket by the side of Molly's bed, and disturbed the squirming little bundle that staggered over to huddle up against the big warm dog. The bundle began to whimper.

'Aunt Molly? Who's that?'

Molly grinned in the dark and shook her head. There was no way out of the tangle. She reached over and snapped on the bedside lamp. There, almost lost in Shag's heavy fur, was a wriggling bundle of puppy barely past the weaning stage.

'That,' Molly announced grandly, 'is your Christmas present.'

Moira squealed in delight and swung herself off the bed. 'A puppy? My own?' There was no sign of tears, or of panic. This was pure childhood joy, and the thoughts of a moment earlier were gone whistling down the wind. And I wish I could do that, Molly told herself. Either forget that strange passage of arms—Tim's arms—or preserve it forever, pressed hard against my heart!

'Your very own,' she said. 'Quiet down, love. It's all yours. Of course, if you'd waited until tomorrow, I would have wrapped him up in a tasty package. But what you see is what you get.'

Moira squealed again, and swept the little brown bundle up in her arms. 'I'm gonna call him—Bertie,' she said. 'My friend Nicole had a dog that she called Bertie, and he was the nicest friend, and that's why I'm gonna call him that!' Molly grinned. The puppy squirmed restlessly and then accepted the new warmth, yawned, and went back to sleep. 'Oh, Aunt Molly,' the little girl sighed, 'how wonderful you are!'

'Yes, aren't I,' Molly returned sceptically. 'Now, get into bed, chum, before you freeze your—little toes off!'

Moira complied with enthusiasm, jumping into Molly's slot in the bed, still cradling the puppy in her arms.

'That animal isn't house-broken,' Molly cautioned in a whisper. 'For heaven's sake calm him down. The whole house needs sleep this night!' The pair, the little girl and the dog, nuzzled each other, and almost instantly fell asleep. The child doesn't know any better, Molly told herself as she watched. Angels, the pair of them. Too bad they have to grow up!

The puppy and the child might not have known that dogs didn't sleep in beds, but Shag did. Nevertheless the big dog whined a couple of times and then, by a gallant effort, elevated himself into all the rest of the bed.

'Shag, you monster!' Molly hissed. The animal buried his head in the blankets and played out of sight, out of mind. 'And thank you all,' Molly muttered as she stole the duvet off the foot of the bed, switched off the bedside lamp, and coiled herself up in the lounge chair by the window.

Tim came down late, as usual. Not the last, but late. Aunt Gerda was at the stove, busy with a pile of wheat-cakes. Moira was at table, one hand on her fork, the other on her puppy. Shag lay on the floor at her feet, hoping for titbits. Molly, nursing a mug of hot coffee, sat in the corner on the window-seat, an island of glumness in a sea of good cheer.

'Good morning, all,' said Tim. Molly winced and ducked her head, expecting him to make some comment about the previous night.

His daughter smiled up at him and signed, 'I love you.' He turned expectantly to Molly, who conspicuously turned her back.

'You didn't sleep well?' Tim walked across the floor to Molly's side and laid one hand gently on her shoulder. She flinched away from him. He snatched the hand away as if it had been burned.

'Your wheat-cakes are ready, Tim,' Aunt Gerda announced.

'Look what Aunt Molly gave me for Christmas!' His daughter was unable to contain herself further. She held the puppy up in both hands and extended it towards her father.

'A dog?' He shook his head, a rueful look on his face. 'That's all we need, baby. With all our travelling from pillar to post, we need a dog like we need a hole in the head!' Moira looked as if she were about to cry, while Aunt Gerda made 'tut-tutting' noises.

But Molly, worn, tired, angry, lost her temper. She swung around on the window seat and glared at him. 'That's it, Tim Holland!' she snapped. 'Think only about yourself, as usual! Damn you!'

'What the devil have *I* done?' he replied forcefully. 'All I did was to say good morning. I even shaved before I came down. Do I have bad breath or something? My lord, when I first came back to Magnolia I thought you hadn't changed a bit, Molly Patterson, but now I see how wrong I was. You were a young grouch in the good old days. Now you're an *old* grouch!'

She jumped to her feet, hands on hips, ready to be the worst of fishwives. 'That's the way!' she shouted angrily. 'Change the subject. Bluster. Do anything but face the truth. That little puppy is a pure-bred German Shepherd. He'll stay with Moira for six months, so that they know each other well, and then we'll send him off to be trained as a Hearing Ear dog!'

'A what?' They were all staring at her now, and there was no way to back out.

'A Hearing Ear dog,' she said very firmly, her voice rising as she spoke from a soft whisper to a shout. 'You know that blind people use Seeing Eye dogs? Well, deaf people have the same sort of problem. They need something or someone to tell them about noises or people behind them, or sirens, or traffic noises. Especially at night, when most hard-of-hearing people take off their hearing aids. And that's when they need a Hearing Ear dog, to alert them to intruders or dangers that they can't hear. To guard them against all comers. And they have them. Hearing Ear dogs, trained to respond to unusual noises, and to alert their owners. Alert and guard them. And that's what this little fellow is. A year from now he'll be a blessing. And I don't give a darn about the inconvenience it might cause you, moving up and down and around Robin Hood's barn!'

'Hey!' protested Tim, a shocked expression on his face. 'Hey, I plead ignorance, Molly. I've never heard of such a thing! But now that you explain, it makes a wonderful amount of sense. I'm sorry, Molly.'

'Yes, I'll bet you are,' she said grimly, unwilling to be conciliated. Best friend Patterson, she snarled at herself, and loathed the thought of it. Right at the moment she was fully prepared to murder her 'best friend'.

'Hey now!' Tim protested as he moved closer, close enough to put an arm around her shoulders. 'Hey now, Moll. You really *didn't* get enough sleep last night, did you?' And then, trying to make a joke of it, 'I finally had to seek help for myself. I haven't slept better in months!'

'I'll bet you did,' she muttered at him. 'I've heard tell that that sort of thing relaxes a man.' Sharply focused in her mind was the picture of Susan watching as she had come out of Tim's room the night before, and the self-satisfied smile on Susan's face.

'Yeah,' he chuckled, 'you're right. It was so good that I tried it twice!'

'Oh, God,' she muttered as tears, rage, and frustration all rose at the same time. With a strength she never knew she possessed she brushed him aside and went running out of the kitchen, her eyes awash. He had just confirmed her worst suspicion. After *she* had left Tim's room, Susan had gone in! And certainly the pair of them hadn't stopped at a handshake! She stopped just long enough at the door to yell a final defiance at him. 'Timothy Holland,' she screamed, 'you are an insensitive, impossibly stupid—oaf!' And with that outburst she shouldered Susan to one side and went charging up the stairs and into her room.

'Well, what was *that* all about?' Petite Susan managed to regain her balance and sauntered into the room, looking the height of fashion in her flouncy semi-transparent négligé.

'I'm damned if I know,' Tim sighed. 'All I did was mention that I took two sleeping pills last night, and she blew her top! That's not like good old Molly! Maybe I'd better——'

'Maybe,' Aunt Gerda suggested pithily, 'you'd better sit down at the table and use your mouth for eating. My lord! You're the smartest Holland of your generation. You're the only male Holland left alive in the world! The rest of them died from terminal stupidity, Timothy—and you'd better see if you can't get an inoculation to save yourself.' At which point Gerda grounded a stack of wheat-cakes in front of him, sniffed in a very superior fashion, and marched smartly out of the room herself.

'I really need some breakfast,' whined Susan.

'Get it yourself,' Tim roared.

'You know I can't cook,' she protested.

'I'll make you some toast,' her daughter promised in a disgusted voice. When she delivered it, each piece was burned on the bottom, but Susan, completely out of her depth but hoping for the best, dared not protest.

Molly came out of hiding at noon. She was thoroughly cried out, and totally ashamed of herself. A short nap had improved her appearance, and now she contemplated the ruin she had created all around her. What a mess! she lectured herself. The only thing you salvaged from the wreckage is that at least you didn't go around blabbing that you loved him! Everything's spoiled. Well, there's no hope for loving, but perhaps—just perhaps—I might work my way back up to friend? With that thought in mind she bundled herself up in workmanlike ski-pants and heavy woollen shirt, and went back downstairs again.

Moira was at the window of the living-room, her nose glued to the glass, watching the snow swirl in the clutches of a rising wind. Gerda sat in the rocking chair, knitting. 'I'm—sorry I made such a fuss,' Molly said.

'No need to apologise,' Aunt Gerda replied. 'He deserved it. If not for what he did last night, then for whatever he's done in the past nine years. I say it again—my nephew is an idiot!

'But that's not important,' Gerda continued. 'What's important is that it's Christmas Eve tonight, and we don't even——' Her voice broke as she waved a hand around the undecorated room.

'Of course,' said Molly. 'You're right. And we have—where's your father, Moira?'

'My nephew is out in the barn trying to do something with that emergency power plant,' Gerda snapped angrily. 'So far today he's managed to shovel a path to the barn, another to the road, and a third to the gazebo on the cliffs. Why would we want a path to the cliffs?'

'Maybe he plans to jump off,' Moira suggested morosely.

'Or perhaps push somebody off,' added Molly, equally glum.

'I don't understand how he could be so brilliant as to make a million—as to make so few mistakes in business,' Gerda complained. 'Why don't you get a baseball bat and go reason with him, Molly.'

'I—might not be welcome,' she stammered. 'Where's—why don't we get Susan to go?'

'Her Royal Pain in the Backside has retired to her room,' Gerda continued. 'It would seem that eating breakfast was just too much for her. Or maybe it was having to wash her own dishes. Any objections?'

'I washed her dishes,' Moira complained. 'Me!'

'No,' laughed Molly, relieved to get out from under all the gloom. 'Well, maybe one. I don't own a bat!'

Aunt Gerda gave her a long glare, snatched up her work and started for the stairs. 'If there's one thing more we don't need,' the older woman announced to her great-niece, 'it's another female smart-mouth! Call me for dinner!'

Moira and Molly stood side by side at the window, looking out, wondering what to do next. The sun was rapidly disappearing, masked by more clouds marching in from the north-east. With a start, Molly looked down to see the child's fingers signing with speed.

'Do you think we'll ever live long enough to have dinner?' the girl signed.

'Never a doubt,' Molly returned. 'Even if it's only K-rations. I'll do it.'

'Do what?'

'I'll go and beard the lion in his den—I mean, in my barn!'

'I don't understand that middle sign,' the child said. 'Board?'

'Beard,' smiled Molly, and repeated the sign for instruction.

'I still don't understand,' Moira sighed. 'Beard the lion?'

'Yes. It's an archaic English expression,' Molly said

with a perfectly straight face. 'It means I'm going to go out there and beat up your father.'

'I could help?'

'No, you stay here. You can be Florence Nightingale.'

'Sure,' Moira agreed. And then, 'You must be awful old, Aunt Molly. What movie did Florence Nightingale play in?'

'Watch my lips,' Molly said solemnly. 'I'm going to teach you to speak a few Italian words. *Shut uppa you mouth, kid!* Got it?'

'Spoilsport!' The girl ducked to avoid the round-house swing which never would have reached her in the first place, and laughed helplessly as her aunt struggled into her outdoor gear.

Tim was bent over the frame of the big Elsen-Gorman generator when Molly stamped into the barn. The one electric light bulb made hardly a dent in the darkness. It was an old barn, with cracks in the walls big enough to let the cold wind squeeze through, and crowded with the haphazard parking of two cars. Now and again he would yell a couple of four-letter words and bang at the power plant with his fist, but he did not realise that Molly had arrived until she touched his shoulder. At that point he swallowed a couple more words, and dropped his screwdriver.

'What the devil are you doing out here?' he yelled at her.

'Looking for you,' she replied. 'Did you know that the wind-chill factor is down to minus twenty degrees?'

'No, I didn't know,' he shouted back over the steady roar of the wind. 'Is there something else I should guess at to win a prize?'

'Don't Tim.' She moved up close to make conversation

possible. 'Don't be sarcastic. All we seem to do is wind each other up these days. At this temperature if you touch that cold metal you'll lose some skin. Please? And tonight's Christmas Eve.'

'That's true, Molly.' He grabbed at an old rag and made a half-hearted attempt to wipe his hands off before he touched her. 'And somehow I get the impression that I've done something I shouldn't?'

'T'other way around,' she said ruefully. 'We both haven't done something we should have. The Christmas tree is over there in the corner.'

'I knew it,' he chuckled. 'I just knew it! Give me another few minutes here and we'll go decorate the tree.'

'Moira would like that,' Molly told him. 'Why don't you leave this old clunker alone?'

'Don't be insulting,' he teased. 'Machines are sensitive to criticism. The engine part here is almost a duplicate of the motors we have on our boats, and I'm sure I can fix it. Another repetition of last night's storm and we'll lose the city power for sure. What the devil is that?'

'That' was a large grumbling noise from outside. Molly went to the door and peered through a crack. 'Well, I'll be darned!' she called. 'A snow-plough! I don't know what to make of that. Usually the DPW doesn't get to us until five or six days after a——'

'After what?' probed Tim, still tinkering at the generator. She walked slowly back to him, hands clasped behind her back.

'Would you believe,' she sighed, 'it was a big blue snow-plough, with Holland Ocean Fisheries printed on the side?'

'I believe,' he grinned, and checked his wrist watch. 'I told them to get it done by three o'clock this afternoon. The power of positive persuasion!'

'You just *suggested* they come plough our street?' she asked softly.

'That's right, Molly Patterson,' he said. 'I called them on the telephone, oh, so politely, and *suggested* they come plough our street.'

'And they did,' she said glumly as she cleared a space on top of an old barrel and sat down. 'Sometimes, Tim, I wish I were rich. You know, real rich. With money to burn, and all that.'

'Well, it *is* the Christmas season,' he said solemnly. 'Here.' He folded something into the palm of her hand. She took a second adjusting to what she held. One small book of paper matches, and one genuine twenty-dollar bill.

'What——' she gasped.

'Hell, live it up,' he growled. 'Lord knows you've been put upon often enough in your young life, Molly. Light the thing up. You've got money to burn!'

'Tim, don't be silly!'

'I'm not being silly,' he insisted. 'Light it up. I'll hold the other end of the bill for you.'

'I couldn't, Tim. Honest, I couldn't!'

'Yes, you can,' he urged. 'Relax. Let it all out. Burn, baby, burn!'

Driven by her own devils, her eyes gleaming in the semi-dark barn, Molly lit a match. Her fingers trembled as she moved the flame closer to the bill. When it flared into fire she yelped so suddenly that Tim almost dropped the burning bill. The pair of them stood and watched until the last fragment was consumed. And they stared at the point where the flame had blossomed, long after it had gone out. Until finally, with a deep sigh, Molly said, 'Lord, that was a wonderful feeling!'

'Do it once a day for two weeks,' he ordered as he bent

over the power plant again.

'Don't be silly,' she muttered, but was attracted to the idea in spite of her New England conscience. And just at that moment the old generator snorted, rumbled, belched, and ran.

Tim watched the fly-wheel turn, a happy smile on his face. He had not for many years looked so boyish, so proud, so sure of himself. Anything that's machinery, she reminded herself. If you tell Tim what it's supposed to do, he'll make it do it!

'Now how about that?' he said in wonder as he reached for her, twirled her around in the air a couple of times, and kissed her most profoundly. It was a very nice kiss, and Molly had been without adult kissing for some time—not counting that wild attack in his bed the night before—since Alfred had cornered her at the Amateur Theatrical Group and done his best for the Sabine women!

'There,' said Tim as he set her down on her feet and inspected her in a very self-satisfied manner.

'There indeed,' Molly whispered, finding it difficult to shake herself back to reality. She wanted to hurry. There would, of course, be a second and a third kiss like that first one, and if she were properly appreciative, maybe a fourth! Despite her high-flying feelings of female independence, she was prepared to grovel just the *slightest* bit to get those extra kisses.

Unfortunately, Tim came down with foot-in-mouth disease at the very moment when he should have been charging forward. 'Let's go get that tree trimmed,' he said.

Moira was standing at the window, her nose hard up against the cold pane, her back turned very firmly towards the only other occupant of the room, her mother. Her puppy was cuddled up in her arms, snoring away with enthusiasm. Snow was beginning to spit again; it looked to be a white Christmas for sure, if only her did and Aunt Molly would come back from the barn.

'Moira, how would you like to come and live with me in New York?' The little girl heard, even though her hearing aid was turned down low, but made no move—gave no indication.

'See here, girl, don't give me *that* nonsense!' Susan had padded across the room, seized her by the shoulder, and whirled her around. They were almost of a size, with Moira shorter by perhaps three inches. 'I said something to you!' Susan snapped.

'I can't hear you,' Moira answered stolidly. 'Did you say something? I'm deaf, you know.'

'I don't know any such a thing,' her mother said shrilly as she shook the child a couple of times, as hard as she could. Moira glared at her.

'I don't know what you want.' She spat the words out one at a time. 'I know you don't want *me*. How would your friends feel if they knew you had a deaf daughter, Mama?'

'Why, you little—monster!' Susan pulled back her open hand, intending to slap the child, when Aunt Gerda bumbled into the room. All three of them froze, like sculptured ice-statues.

'I'm sure I'm not seeing what I'm seeing,' the round little elderly lady said coldly. 'I wouldn't want to see anyone lay a hand on that child. Anyone!'

'I can do what I like with my daughter,' Susan snapped.

'And I can tell Tim all about it,' Gerda added gently. 'Can you imagine what he'd do? Why, look, here they come now.'

'And they're dragging a Christmas tree,' Moira said excitedly. 'I didn't think——'

'Your aunt Molly would never forget the Christmas tree,' Gerda laughed. 'A very well-organised woman, your aunt. Very—pragmatic, I think the word is. And full of love.'

Susan tugged at Moira's arm. 'We'll talk again,' she whispered. 'Don't forget. It would be a shame for anything to happen to your sweet little dog. Ugh! Get that animal out of my face!'

Torn between pain and passion, Moira brushed her mother aside and ran for the back door. The pair outside had stopped for a moment for a snowball fight. One of them had terrible aim; the missile missed Tim, and came sailing up to bang off the open door just above Moira's head. 'Hey, you two,' the child yelled, 'if that's the best you can do, I'll beat you both!'

'Not a chance,' gasped Molly as she stumbled up on to the porch, leaving Tim to struggle with the tree. 'We have to get this decorated before supper. All the ornaments are in the hall closet, love. Why don't you start bringing them out while your father—not there, Tim! For goodness' sake, you know very well we *always* put the tree in the corner of the living-room!'

The rest of the afternoon was filled with noises, movement, laughter, teasing and love, as Tim and Molly did the high decorations, Gerda supervised, and Moira tied the light-strings around the lower branches. Shag even added to the excitement. He came in, thumped down beside Gerda, and took over as the puppy's nanny. Of Susan there was no sign.

At five o'clock it was dark outside. The storm still threatened, but had not yet delivered. The old snow, twelve to fourteen inches deep in flat areas, four to five feet high in drifts against the windward sides of the houses, was enough to keep everyone in Magnolia house-locked. 'WBZ Radio says more snow,' Moira reported as she came back in from the kitchen with a handful of pretzels 'to hold me over until suppertime'.

'I couldn't lift a finger if it did,' Tim reported. He was sprawled out, half in and half out of the big armchair that once had been Molly's father's favourite possession. 'I have digged all I intend to dig.'

'Dug,' Molly signed to Moira, who laughed. 'He speaks English poorly!'

'Cut that out,' Tim ordered. 'We'll have no more of those finger-painting conversations.'

'You only have to learn the language yourself to be up to date,' Molly teased. 'Your daughter is learning like a house on fire. Here, learn this one.' She walked over in front of him and smiled while she signed, 'I love you.'

'I remember that,' he chuckled. 'That's good day, right?'

'Right,' Molly and Moira chimed in at the same time. Gerda, who knew a little better than that, started to giggle. With painful slowness, looking directly at Molly, Tim repeated the signs. *So there*, Molly told herself. *I got him to say it, after all these years. Too bad he doesn't mean it, or even understand what he said!*

Tim sank back in his chair. 'The tree looks wonderful,' he commented. 'Just like it used to. Did you know, Moira, that I spent most of my Christmases over here with Molly when I was your age?'

'It must have been fun,' his daughter said. 'Did your mum and dad come too?'

'Not exactly,' he sighed. 'My mother—wasn't with us too often at Christmas, and my dad, he—do you remember the story I told you in Paris about Ebenezer

Scrooge?'

'Bah, humbug,' Moira laughed.

'That's the very man,' Molly encouraged her.

'That was your grandfather to a T,' Tim added solemnly. 'Bah, humbug! He didn't believe in Christmas.'

'I know he was my brother,' Aunt Gerda interjected, 'but he didn't even believe in people, God rest him. Well, suppose we eat? I don't know any ceremony that can't be improved by a good meal!'

'I'll call Susan,' Molly offered, then looked down at the child, busy trying to appear invisible. 'While Moira gets washed, right?'

'I'm gonna wear away,' the little girl complained. 'Every time I turn around somebody wants me to get washed. My skin is going to peel away and turn into gills or something!'

'*Git*,' her father commanded. She got, snatching up her puppy as she went by Shag, and taking the stairs two at a time.

'We really need another bathroom,' Molly sighed as she watched.

'Well, that certainly fits into the conversation,' laughed Tim, as Molly started up the stairs, much more slowly. She found Susan sitting by the telephone in the upstairs hall. The woman had a smirk on her face as she concluded her conversation and restored the instrument to its cradle.

'Just a minute, Molly,' she called as her cousin started to turn into her own bedroom. She rose gracefully and took the two steps that brought them face to face. What big teeth you have, Grandmother, Molly thought apropos nothing. More like a shark than a grandmother!

'I'm sure Tim told you why I came all the way up here,' Susan said blandly.

'I can't say that he did,' Molly replied. 'I suppose he thought it was none of my business.'

'Perhaps. But there is a part of it that concerns you.'

'Oh, yes?'

'Yes, cousin.' There was the tiniest barb on that last word, or perhaps a calling in of favours due to a relative? Molly cocked her head to one side and prepared for the storm. 'I came up here to talk over Moira's position in the world,' Susan continued. 'That was something not settled by the divorce decree. Usually the mother gets custody, especially when it's a daughter, you know.'

'Oh?' A very weak *oh* at that, Molly chided herself. The whole idea was a surprise to her. Susan might get custody of the child? Good lord! She was so astonished that she missed the next few words of the one-way conversation.

'—and we'd scheduled a meeting with my lawyer,' Susan was saying, 'only of course with travelling so difficult and all—well, it's almost impossible for us to go to his office. But we're lucky.'

'Yes, of course we are,' Molly sighed, still not sure where the conversation was headed. 'Why are we lucky?'

'Because he lives up here in Manchester,' Susan explained. 'Isn't that nice? Now he's agreed to drive over here tonight, you see, and Tim and I and the lawyer can sit down together and iron the whole thing out. Wouldn't that be nice?'

'Yes, of course,' Molly repeated, still feeling fuzzy about the whole affair, and wondering what in the world was going on.

'But with the storm coming in again,' Susan said hurriedly, 'he might not be able to drive back to Manchester, so we would have to invite him to stay the night.'

Relieved to have finally arrived at some sensible point, Molly nodded her head, managed a half-smile, and said, 'Certainly. Did you invite him?'

'Well, to tell the truth I did.' Susan was displaying that little feline smile that meant trouble. Molly had seen it many times before, but people from downstairs were calling, something about the supper being on the table, and she missed the cue.

'Come on.' She held out her hand to Susan. After all, it was Christmas Eve, the woman *was* her cousin, and forgive and forget, wasn't that what Christianity was all about? On their way back down the stairs they scooped up Moira, looking just the slightest bit more neat than when she had come up, and the three of them walked into the kitchen together.

CHAPTER SEVEN

IT WAS a pick-up supper. Molly contributed spaghetti and meatballs and a bottled tomato sauce. Aunt Gerda added a Jello dessert, stuffed with canned fruits, and a home-made loaf of garlic bread. Tim brought a large appetite to the dining-room table; Moira provided an excess of excitement. And Susan sat in the middle of all the action, doing nothing, but smiling that weird smile—like a vampire waiting for the clock to strike, Molly told herself.

What really nagged her was that Tim was devoting most of his time to his ex-wife. 'He should be giving some attention to his daughter,' she muttered to Gerda as they passed each other on the way to the stove. What she meant was, he should be giving *me* some attention! She didn't have to tell Gerda that. The elderly lady seemed to be the only one in the room who understood all the players and all the rules.

When Molly staggered into the dining-room with the huge platter of spaghetti, Tim came to the door to help. 'You got him!' Moira yelled.

'Got who?' asked Molly puzzled. Tim had both hands on one end of the platter, while Molly had her hands on the other.

'The mistletoe!' Moira shrieked excitedly. Both Tim and Molly looked up at the same time. Some misguided soul had hung a sprig of holly and mistletoe above them in the middle of the doorway. Molly did her best to back up, but her fingers held fast to the plate, and Tim refused to give ground. In fact, egged on by cheering from the table, he pulled the platter in his direction, and before Molly could gather her flustered senses, his warm moist lips were on her own. For a moment she felt the pure bliss of it all. A small triumph, surely, but for a girl whose triumphs were few and far between, this kiss was an overwhelming success.

'Yeah man, go!' yelled Moira.

'How lovely,' Aunt Gerda commented as she inched Shag away from the table with the toe of her shoe.

'Don't drop the spaghetti,' Susan warned disgustedly.

It was that last comment that shocked Molly back to sensibility. 'Don't Tim,' she objected, pulling her head back.

'You never used to object to a mistletoe kiss,' he murmured.

No, Molly thought, but in those days I hadn't dreamed of Susan coming out of your bedroom, nor heard you boasting about *doing it twice,* for heaven's sake! Even a best friend has to be sensible about some things. Especially sex. 'Take the platter to the table,' she told him firmly, and turned back to the kitchen for the sauce.

Determined not to put a damper on the Christmas Eve celebration, when Molly came out of the kitchen on her last trip she came with a smile and a joke. There was no argument about who had what place; the table was round, and big enough to hold half a dozen additional people.

Aunt Gerda was at her best too, recalling a dozen or more stories about the 'old days,' when Molly and Tim had been known as the Disaster Duo. Moira hung on her every word. Susan could hardly keep from yawning. And the two alleged participants ducked and dodged and blushed—but could hardly deny the truth of most of the tales.

So the meal ended in good spirits. As they transferred to the living-room they could hear a car driving up outside. Moira ran to the door. The incipient storm was only a threat, but it was still a difficult driving time. The visitor was receiving a warm welcome. There was a suitable delay to allow the discarding of boots and overcoat, then Moira danced into the living-room, hand in hand with—Captain Josiah Francis!

'I didn't think I'd make it,' the Captain said as he walked directly across to the fireplace and rubbed his hands in front of the gas-blaze. 'Comin' up to storm again. Did I miss anything?'

'Spaghetti, Captain Ahab,' Moira chimed in. He turned and laughed down at her.

'You're the cute little piece I met with Molly, aren't you. Molly?'

'Right here, Captain. It's wonderful to see you on Christmas Eve, but did I forget I'd invited you?'

'*I* invited him,' said Gerda, moving up to take the Captain's arm. 'I couldn't bear to think of the poor man all alone on a night like this.'

'Besides, we've been sharing Christmas for years,' the Captain chuckled. 'Did I spoil something? Make the numbers wrong?'

'Nothing like that,' Molly said cheerfully. 'And we were about to be hopelessly short of men around these parts. Have you eaten?'

'Done that already,' he told her. 'Do I put these presents under the tree?'

'I'll take them, Josiah,' said Tim. The two men shook hands in a bone-breaking clasp that illustrated a considerable friendship. The Captain unloaded his pockets, then spied Susan.

'I don't believe I've had the pleasure,' he said.

'Ah. Susan, this is Captain Francis, the Commodore of our fleet.'

'And I'm Tim's wife,' Susan announced as she came around the table.

'So.' The Captain looked quickly at Gerda, and evidently received some signal. He nodded his head and said, 'And what brings you to these parts, little lady?'

Susan took his other arm. 'I think I was cheated on the division of the spoils,' she told him. 'My lawyer and I are looking into the situation. And of course, I just *had* to see my daughter, you know. Mother love is a strong urge!'

'I wouldn't know much about that,' the Captain said gruffly as he turned around to Molly. 'I don't know that I'll be able to drive back tonight, Miss Molly,' he continued. 'Would it be inconvenient for me to stay over?'

'Of course it wouldn't' said Aunt Gerda, and gave Molly a guilty look.

'Of course it wouldn't,' Molly repeated. 'Sit over here, Josiah. Are you sure we couldn't offer you something to eat?'

'Nope,' he declined. 'Had me a big supper earlier, up to Gloucester. Never go on a trip without a good meal beforehand, that's my motto. Who in the world is *that* comin' up?' Another car motor had sounded outside, a horn tooted, and brakes squealed.

Tim pulled back the lace curtain and peered out into the gloom. 'Can't see a thing,' he reported. 'The snow's out to make a record for itself. Coming straight down, and big flakes.'

'I'll go,' Susan announced, to everyone's surprise. 'I'm expecting my lawyer, Molly, if you remember?'

'Oh—yes,' Molly replied. 'I'd almost forgotten.' Round and round in her mind a little equation was playing. Seven people, probably to spend the night, and only six bedrooms free. Oh, wow! She looked around the room in desperation. Tim and Moira were eyeing each other, and making some small talk over Bertie. Aunt Gerda and Captain Francis were exchanging messages like long-lost lovers. *Lovers*? *At their age*? *And why not*! Which left Molly and Shag to stare at each other, listening faintly to the very effusive welcome Susan was offering to the latecomer.

It took longer for this newest guest to shed his outer garments. Or maybe Susan had to have a private consultation? Molly asked herself. None of this makes sense. Susan wants——what? Custody of Moira? That was what the verbal communication indicated, but underneath all the words there was something different at stake. What Susan wanted, Molly thought, beyond any doubt, was more money. Or could it be——oh, lord! Molly took a deep breath to try to assuage the sudden pain that had struck her just under her heart. Could it be that Susan wanted it all——wanted Tim back again? If so, she would use *any* manoeuvre to achieve her goal!

So by the time Susan came back into the dining-room, her lawyer behind her, Molly had set her face in an uncompromising judgemental frown, which was almost instantly knocked off.

'People,' Susan said as she walked in, 'I want you to meet my lawyer, Alfred DeMoins!'

Oh, my God, Molly screamed at herself. Oh, my God! And while Susan was leading the lawyer around the room, making introductions, Molly was struggling with her stomach, trying to keep from the final social disgrace. Al DeMoins! The one man in all the millions who lived along the North Shore whom she not only never wanted to meet again, but had fervently prayed that their original meeting might be washed off the records by the Recording Angel!

'Well now, whom have we here?' Al DeMoins. As handsome as a girl's dream, his little individual defects swallowed up in the whole. Five foot ten or so, a little more rotund than he had been during their high-school days, a full head of brown hair that might possibly not be entirely his own. Alfred DeMoins, the man Molly had finally concluded could be the one with whom she might share her first sexual adventure, until, at the last minute, she had discovered just what sort of barracuda he was!

'Hello, Alfred.' Tim's head snapped up as he heard Molly make that dismally discouraging greeting.

'Molly Patterson, I do declare!' Alfred's lips were just a little too full, his tones a little too ripe. 'Our newest heiress! Did you know I've been looking all over Cape Ann for you?'

'No, I didn't know.' Molly clamped her mouth shut. It hadn't been easy, keeping out of Al's way. Not only had she given up all her local friendships, but she had also withdrawn from the job she really loved, teaching. And all because Al DeMoins thought that Molly Patterson owed him something!

'Heiress?' queried Tim, coming around the table to stand at Molly's side.

'Yes,' Alfred replied. 'Won a bundle in the State Lottery, started out to be the Playgirl of the Western World, then disappeared. Dropped completely out of sight! Well, am I glad I found you again, Moll. You owe me.'

'Don't call me that,' she snapped. 'Only my friends call me that.'

'Ah. Of course,' he chuckled. 'And I'm more than a friend, aren't I, Molly P?'

'And don't call her *that* either,' Tim said flatly as he put one arm around Molly's shoulder. It was the nicest thing that had happened to Molly in a month of Sundays. She leaned back against Tim's solid frame and found her courage instantly restored.

'Yeah, Molly and I had some interesting nights,' Alfred boasted.

'*One* interesting night,' Molly stated. 'And I was lucky I had enough mad money to get me home, Mr DeMoins.'

'We'll just have to pick things up where we left off,' he commented.

'I don't think so,' said Tim, and there was something in his voice that caused the lawyer to blink his eyes and look twice.

Alfred licked his dry lips, and tried another attack. 'Staking a claim?' he asked. 'I saw her first.'

'The hell you did!' Tim retorted angrily. 'Molly's been my girl since she was in her cradle. You're not making a social call, DeMoins. You're here on sufferance as Susan's lawyer. Now why don't you and your client come along to the den with me, and we can get down to business. Maybe you can be back to town in an hour or so.'

'I don't think so,' Susan interrupted. 'The snow is really piling up out there. In another few minutes nobody will be able to drive. I think Al will have to spend the night.'

Tim shrugged his shoulders. 'Maybe,' he grated. 'That will be Molly's decision; it's her house. Come on!'

He led the way out of the dining-room, with Alfred hard to his heels. But Susan delayed long enough to glare at Molly. Moira, her puppy in her arms, went over to stand beside her adopted aunt. 'Listen,' Susan hissed, 'don't think a couple of odd remarks have won you any prize,

Molly. You may be my cousin, but Tim is my husband! You couldn't keep him all those years ago, and there's no way I'm going to let you have him now!' And then, turning to her daughter, 'Get that dirty animal away from me, girl! Don't you know anything about hygiene?' With which she shared a glare equally among all the members still standing in the dining-room, and followed her lawyer out into the hall.

'Well!' Aunt Gerda managed a weak little laugh as she moved a few inches closer to the Captain.

'She's mean,' said Moira. 'How could Bertie be dirty? I gave him a bath just this afternoon!'

'Not to worry,' Molly replied. 'There are some people who can't tell clean from dirty, physically or mentally! How about let's finish up our dessert, and then we'll turn on the tree lights, and then——'

'And then we'll all go to bed and wait for Santa Claus to come,' Moira said happily. ''Course, I don't believe in Santa Claus, 'cause I know he's my dad, but——'

'I know,' Molly agreed. 'But on the odd chance that there might be a present or two, you're willing to suspend your disbelief for just one night?'

'Aunt Molly,' the child said suspiciously, 'sometimes you sound more like a kid than a grown-up!'

Eleven o'clock, Christmas Eve. Moira had given up the ghost at ten, worn out by the events of the day. Captain Francis had volunteered to carry her upstairs, where Aunt Gerda had slipped her into her winter nightgown and tucked her in.

Molly had managed to do the dishes and clean up the kitchen, and now she was back in the living-room, her feet drawn up beneath her on the sofa. The wind had risen again, until a glimpse outside indicated that it was snowing sideways. The house rattled and groaned, like an old ship riding the high seas.

The Christmas tree, almost touching the high ceiling, and fastened into its corner in three directions, seemed to rock with every attack of the gale outside. The two dozen little fairy lights blinked, and the angel perched at the very top was dancing. But it had done its duty. The child had been enchanted by the whole affair. When Tim came back from his conference, with Susan and her lawyer close behind, Molly told him about it.

He dropped on to the sofa at her side, which was another plus. The sofa was one of those two-person love-seats. But Tim was somewhat more than one person, and, as a result, he crowded next to her very comfortably. Susan sneered at them both as she sank into one of the armchairs, leaving Alfred to struggle with one of the straight-backs.

'I wouldn't be surprised,' mused Tim. 'We've been a pair of wandering gypsies, with no real place to call our home. I mean to make that up to her.'

And I'll help, Molly thought, but kept her mouth shut. Best friends don't go around making statements like that. Tim was so obviously gun-shy that a single wifely remark like that might send him off and running again!

'Strange child,' Alfred chimed in. 'I never thought, years ago, when I first met Susan, that she would have a child like that.'

'Oh? You knew Susan years ago?' Tim was about as casual as a man could be, which meant, Molly told herself, that there's something in the wind here. That casual *bon vivant* role was his best act! She sat up a little straighter to follow the conversation.

'Yes indeed,' Alfred rambled on. 'I knew Susan back in her salad days, so to speak.' The man was just far enough away from the little blonde so that her attempt to kick his ankle failed. Molly marked that down and filed it in her capacious memory.

Tim got up and refilled the lawyer's brandy glass. It wasn't for the first time, and Alfred was showing evidence of having been to the well too often. Susan, giving every evidence of a woman about to have a screaming fit, just could not get his attention.

'And deafness too,' the lawyer wandered on. 'Isn't that funny? We have a lot of that in my family. My aunt and my sister both came down with it. Some sort of congenital defect, I understand. All in the female side, it seems. Luckily it skipped me.'

'You surely are lucky,' Tim agreed affably. 'It would be pretty hard lawyering if you were deaf. What do you think about that, Susan?'

'I think I'm going to bed,' she hissed at them, her face red with fury. 'Did you find a bed for Alfred?'

'Yes, indeed,' Molly told her. 'Moira and I are doubling up in my big bed, and Mr DeMoins can have her room. Would you show him, Susan?'

'I'll show him *something*,' Susan retorted. For the first time Al realised that he had his foot in his mouth. He followed the other woman out, his face red as a beet.

'Now what do you suppose *that* was all about,' asked Tim as he came back to the sofa and squeezed in beside her. He was wearing his most innocent expression, but Molly had been down that route too many times in the past.

'Tell me about it,' she murmured. His arm came around her shoulders and settled in. 'You know darned well what. Al DeMoins knew Susan a long time ago. Al DeMoins comes from a family that has hereditary problems with deafness. Two and two make——'

'Five,' he interrupted, laying a finger across her lips. 'Listen to me carefully, friend Molly, because this is the first and last time I expect the subject to come up. Moira is *my* daughter, and I shall love and cherish her as long as I live—no matter who her natural father is. Got that, have you?'

Molly gulped. The pressure of his finger on her lips was the lightest of touches; the pressure of his look, gleaming out of a pale determined face, bore all the weight of years. 'Yes,' she whispered, 'I've got that!'

They sat silently for a while, savouring the warmth, the brightness of the Christmas lights, the soft sound from radio station WBZ, broadcasting carols. The wind dropped off, but the snow continued, piling flake on flake in its inexorable attempt to shut off human life. Finally she stirred.

'Early morning, Tim. Remember? Moira will be up at the crack of dawn, ready to open her presents. Everything's in the hall closet. How about bringing the packages out while I hang the stockings?'

'Mrs Kringle, I take it,' he chuckled. 'OK. And while I'm at it, I'll shake out a little hay for the reindeer.'

'Don't you dare!' She shuddered in mock fear. 'All the hay's in the barn. If you try to go out there tonight we'll need two St Bernard dogs just to *find* you.'

'I'll be careful,' he promised jokingly. 'St Bernards were the dogs that carried the brandy casks around their necks to sustain the lonely traveller, weren't they?'

'Don't look at *me* like that. I don't have anything around my neck for you, Tim Holland!'

'Well, you could have fooled me.' And me too, Molly told herself. For there was something around her neck—both his hands, gently caressing, pulling her forward until her breasts flattened against his shirt-front, her nose buried at about the third button of his shirt. Her arms stole around his waist—well, as far around as they could reach.

The hug was gentle, as brotherly as one might expect. But when he tilted her chin up and kissed her there was nothing brotherly about that. Nothing at all. For what seemed like hours he punished her with delight, until she clung desperately, breathless.

'And just what was that all about?' she gasped at last as he relented and set her an inch or two away from him.

'For old times' sake,' he murmured.

Please don't tell me that, Molly thought wildly. Not anything about the good old days. *These* are the good old days, Tim Holland. I've never had it so good. I've never been kissed with such—enthusiasm. I've never dreamed such dreams as now. And then he lowered the boom.

'You have to help me, Molly.'

'With what?' Barely a whisper, that. She was still caught up in his magic.

'With Susan and her stupid lawyer,' he sighed. 'I think I have everything fixed up. I have a French divorce, and an absolute settlement in writing. But I suppose an American lawyer could pick some little hole in the structure. I mind losing money, just for the principle of the thing, but I could live with a money loss. What I can't live with is the idea that she might be able to take Moira away from me.'

'You know that I'll do anything I can,' Molly answered. 'I love that little girl—' *almost as much as I love her father*! '—but I don't know just what I can do.'

'There are two things,' he suggested hesitantly. 'For the short term, just be nice to the pair of them. As nice as you can possibly be?'

'I guess I could do that. It won't be the easiest thing in

the world, but if I can just keep my temper—What else?'

'Well,' he stammered, as if the words were stuck in his throat, 'the biggest problem is that a court generally tends to give custody to the mother, especially if the father hasn't remarried. It's that bit about how much better a mother can raise a daughter than a father can.'

'So?' Molly swallowed. Her throat was dry, and her mind tingled with anticipation. 'You plan to get married, Tim?'

'Yeah,' he grunted. 'For Moira's sake, of course.'

'Of course. Do I know the lucky woman?'

'Molly?' He took a step or two away from her, then came back, his face under stern control. 'Molly, you don't sound as if you think she'd be all that lucky.'

'How can I tell, Tim? Maybe she's hard up.' *Like me, you fool*! 'Maybe she's nursed a secret passion for you since she was ten years old?' *Or perhaps even six*? 'Or on the other hand, maybe she's waiting around for some words like love and devotion and happy ever after. Has she given you any hope?'

'Not directly,' he muttered. 'But Aunt Gerda says——'

'Aha! A conspiracy? Tell me about it, Tim.'

He took a deep breath and stared down at her with an unfathomable look. 'No,' he sighed, 'I guess I'd better not. I don't think you're ready to hear what I've got to say. Where did you say those presents were?'

'In the hall closet,' she replied, and turned abruptly away from him so he could not see the tears in her eyes.

Luckily her bed was wide. Moira was coiled up on the far side, next to the wall, with little Bertie beside her on her pillow. Shag complained when he was shooed off the other side of the bed. He clumped his way over to the door and stretched out on the throw-rug there. Moira's night-light had been moved to Molly's room. It cast a ruby sheen over everything.

Molly coiled up in her armchair by the window and stared out. Although it was dark outside, it was the reflective darkness of a snowfield, just enough light to show the big flakes drifting down. Behind her, she could hear Shag's heavy breathing. We're getting old, my dog and I, she thought. For a moment there tonight I thought I had a hand on the brass ring. But close is a measure only good while playing horseshoes.

Poor dumb, beautiful Tim! How can such an intelligent, lovable man be so stupid about women? I wonder, is it a *new* woman he's talking about, or can he be so foolish as to take up with Susan again? How in heaven's name could Alfred DeMoins be Moira's father? Al was in law-school when Tim and Susan were married, and he didn't graduate until two years later. Which left practically no time for him to zoom over to Europe and do the dirty deed! And Aunt Gerda! I was almost positive she was on *my* side, but no, that pair—the Captain and Gerda—are deep in a conspiracy to—to whatever. If I were in my right mind I go down the hall and wake Gerda up right now, and demand an answer!

Putting action to words, Molly slipped into her heavy winter robe and her fur-lined slippers. Shag protested at the opening of the door. So much disturbed was the old dog that he padded down the hall after her, breathing heavily. A few chains to rattle, and he'd make a great ghost, Molly thought as she gently turned the doorknob and opened Gerda's door.

There was practically no light at all in Aunt Gerda's room. Molly stumbled across the rug by the bed, and shook the covers. 'Gerda?' No response. 'Gerda!' Still no answer.

Determined to have her way, Molly felt across the top blanket, ready to shake a shoulder—or whatever else she came across. She leaned so far across the bed that eventually she slipped and fell flat on her face. But her nose, her hands, questing, returned the same message. Aunt Gerda was not in her bed. A moment later when Molly managed to turn on the bedlamp the conclusion was unavoidable. Aunt Gerda was not in her room!

Nonplussed, Molly sat down on the edge of the bed. 'Here's a how-de-do?' she whispered. Only W.S. Gilbert could provide the words for her present situation. Aunt Gerda was—perhaps sixty years old? Not too old, of course. Not too old for what? her conscience demanded. Maybe she's in the bathroom? Not too old for Captain Francis, who was about the same age, and as spry an elderly man as could ever be seen!

Being a true optimist, and stuffed to the gills with curiosity, Molly stopped off to inspect the empty bathroom, and almost fell over Shag, who was sitting patiently outside the door. So Aunt Gerda was missing, in the middle of the wildest snowstorm since the blizzard of '88. 1888, that was.

I can't spot-check the house, Molly told herself. Besides, everyone except Moira is an adult, and if they all want to play at adultery, what business is that of mine? Nevertheless, when she went by Susan's door, she stuck out her determined chin and tried again. There was a little light in Susan's room, a reflection from the hall lights. And once again an empty bed.

A hysterical little giggle rose in her throat. I worried about having enough beds for everyone, she told herself, and here I already have two empties! Quit while you're ahead, kid! She pulled her robe more tightly around her and headed for her own room. Shag had beaten her to the bed; she had to shoo him off again. He went reluctantly.

Molly slid gently under the sheets, trying not to disturb the little girl. Warmth enveloped her, and she became drowsy. I wonder, she thought, if Tim is still in *his* assigned bed? For a moment she thought to check, but when she moved one toe out from under the covers the cold shocked her, and she changed her mind. 'Besides,' she whispered, 'I don't really want to know. Well, I really do, but I don't dare to know. It's Christmas morning, and I have to wake up early to be with Moira.' With which thought she fell into a troubled sleep.

CHAPTER EIGHT

THERE was no dawn on Christmas Day. Heavy clouds hung over all the north shore of Massachusetts, but the snow had stopped. As expected, Moira was up at the first sign of light, and Molly, sharing the bed, was forced to join her in the mad dash downstairs. The house rang with the child's excited shouts, and not all the householders were pleased.

'Can't you keep that kid quiet?' grumbled Alfred as he came downstairs, bleary-eyed, at seven in the morning. By that time Moira had picked over the pile of presents under the tree, shredded the paper on those marked for her, and was marching up and down with her puppy tagging along behind, and a huge Snoopy doll in her arms. It was amazing to see how her shyness and reserve had vanished under a landslide of love.

'I'm sure we could,' Molly responded coldly, 'but who wants to?'

'I do,' Alfred snapped. 'If I were her father I'd slap her bottom good!'

'If you were her father,' Molly replied tersely, 'she'd deserve it. There's coffee on the stove, toast on the table, and scrambled eggs on the sideboard.'

'I have croissants with my coffee,' he complained as he sat down.

'Tough,' Aunt Gerda said sarcastically.

'You don't look too bad,' Molly told the elderly lady as the pair of them turned their backs on the lawyer. He gave them a disgusted look and walked out into the living-room.

'Too bad for what?'

'Well, I went looking for you just after midnight,' Molly chuckled, and Aunt Gerda blushed.

'I'm a little old,' she replied, 'but I'm not dead. Not yet, Miss Prude. Why did you want me?'

'It doesn't matter now,' Molly sighed. 'I'd been talking to Tim. He seemed to suggest that you and he were involved in a conspiracy to get him married again. He didn't appear too enthusiastic, and it didn't concern me, so——'

'Conspiracy?' Gerda interrupted her. 'And it didn't concern you?' Molly shook her head. 'I can see why you would think things are confused,' Aunt Gerda said. 'But it that's all the explaining Tim is ready to do, I'm sure I ought to keep my mouth shut about it. Did you know that Captain Francis comes to spend the holidays with me at Christmas, Easter, and the Fourth of July?'

'Does he really?' smiled Molly. 'Have a good time, do you?'

Aunt Gerda grinned broadly. 'The best,' she chuckled. 'Celibacy isn't all it's cracked up to be.'

'I wouldn't know,' sighed Molly. 'Somehow or another I just seemed to be too busy to—well, to find out.'

'You couldn't find a better time,' Gerda teased. 'Snowbound like this? Now's your chance. Hop upstairs and make your selection.'

'I couldn't do it,' Molly replied glumly. 'Yours wasn't the only bed I checked on last night. Although I didn't run into anyone, it seems to me that the traffic up and down that hall must have been something fierce. If I could have sold toll tickets, I might have made a bundle. But my courage failed, and I went back to my own bed.'

'Poor baby,' the older woman said. 'Pass me the

coffee-pot again.'

Tim chose that moment to poke his head in from the living-room, where he had been sharing Christmas with his daughter. 'Ho, ho, ho,' he chortled. 'Why do I see gloomy faces in the kitchen?'

'Bah, humbug,' Molly told him. 'Did you have enough breakfast?'

'I did,' he reported. 'Who gave me this—astounding—necktie?'

'The one with the yellow dragon breathing fire? I thought it was most appropriate,' Molly said primly. 'It about matches the green shawl you gave me, the one with the three can-can dancers on it.'

'Hey, the bell has sounded. That's the end of round one,' Gerda laughed. 'Back to your corners. Alfred, did you eat all the toast?'

'Who, me?' the lawyer looked up at them all through bleary eyes. Plainly he had nipped at the brandy bottle after he had gone up to bed as well as before. 'We need to talk some more, Holland.'

'No, I don't think so,' Tim answered nonchalantly. 'After thinking it over I think my answer is not only no, but hell, no! Not a penny more. And the first person who makes any threat about *my daughter*——' the words hung explosively in the air between them '——will find it very detrimental to his health. Or hers, as the case may be. Now, how about some more toast, Aunt Gerda?'

About a mile north of the house, at just that moment, in the middle of Norman Avenue, Billy Sunderson was making a stupidly gallant effort to deliver a late Christmas present. As he came up to the crossroads at Ocean Avenue a dog ran out into his path. He slammed on his brakes, skidded across the intersection, turned around twice, and smashed the back end of his truck into the power pole on the corner. The pole shifted, the hot wires at its peak snapped, and half the village of Magnolia lost its power. Including the old house on the bluff overlooking Kettle Cove.

'Oh, damn!' grumbled Tim. Everyone in the kitchen waited. There was an automatic switch out in the barn which was supposed to turn on the emergency generator when the main power went off. Nothing happened.

'Oh, damn,' Tim repeated as he got up and searched for his work clothes among the heap of jackets by the back door. 'I'll have to shovel my way to the barn and turn the thing on by hand.'

'I'll help,' Molly offered. Alfred came back into the kitchen and sat down stolidly in his chair, with never a thought of helping.

'I can't shovel. My back, you know, but the Captain can,' Aunt Gerda volunteered. 'I'll call him.'

'No, don't wake him up,' Tim objected. 'Molly and I can handle this. Why don't you recruit some help and check on the lanterns, the gas fires—things like that. Will the furnace run without electricity, Molly?'

'I hope so,' she groaned. 'It's supposed to. But then the emergency power is supposed to work too. Come on.'

'Papa, can I come too?' Little Moira, ready to give up the warmth for a romp outside.

He was about to say no when Molly nudged him in the back. 'Yes, of course you can,' he agreed. 'But get bundled up. And you have to leave your dog inside, you know. Puppies aren't quite ready for sub-zero snowstorms. Aunt Gerda will help you.'

'That was a good thing to do,' Molly told him after she caught her first breath of frozen air. 'I think I'll just wrap this scarf around my nose too.'

'What, even with the can-can girls on it?' he laughed.

'Don't be indelicate,' she told him gloomily. 'Take up thy shovel and walk, man.'

'And where are you going to start?'

'I'm directing,' she chuckled. 'Me chief, you Indian. Get with it!'

'Well, you just said the magic word.' He handed her his shovel, tipped his fur cap jauntily over one eye, and stepped off the back porch.

'Tim Holland, you dirty rat,' she screamed at him with her best James Cagney imitation. 'You come back here and shovel!'

'You're not supposed to shout at daddies like that,' Moira said from behind her back. The little girl was swaddled in every conceivable kind of warm clothing, and clutched a toy shovel in her mittened hands.

'He's not *my* daddy,' Molly grumbled. 'Tim Holland, you come back here!'

'I'm doing just what you said,' he called. 'Walk! It's power we want, not paths. The snow's only at my knees along here. You two shovel while I just plough my way over and get the generator started!'

'Now why didn't I think of that?' Molly asked her partner in shovelling.

'I dunno,' said Moira. 'How can you talk sign language with mittens on?'

'You can't,' Molly laughed. 'It won't work in the dark, either. C'mon, let's shovel like good little girls.'

'You're not,' the child said as she started to work.

'I'm not what?' Molly was already out of breath, and the path was exactly four inches wide—and not likely to get any wider.

'You're not little, and you're not a girl,' Moira teased. 'I dunno about bein' good. My daddy says you're the goodest person in the world.'

'Well,' drawled Molly, her shovel moving the slighest bit faster. 'Tell me more! What else does your daddy say?'

'No, sirree,' Moira giggled. 'I'm no blabbermouth. What's that noise?'

Molly stood up to rest her aching back. 'I must be getting old,' she muttered. 'That noise, young lady, is your smart-guy father getting the generator going.'

'So we don't hafta shovel any further?'

'Farther,' Molly corrected. 'No, we don't have to shovel any farther. He can come back the same way he went out—Shanks's pony.'

'Well, in that case,' warned Moira, 'you'd better duck!'

Molly smiled to herself. Another crack had appeared in the child's wall. And where there was tolerance there could be love?

The snowball war lasted about ten minutes before Tim appeared on the horizon like an invading army of Huns, and swept the field. The three of them tumbled into the kitchen moments later, cheeks as red as MacIntoshe apples, their breath steaming in the warmth.

'Dear God,' Susan shrieked, 'shut that door! I don't want to freeze! What in the world were you doing out there in the snow, Tim?'

'And a good morning to you too,' he said grandly, hugging his two helpers. 'I had to turn the electricity back on. Molly forgot to pay the bill!'

'I don't doubt that,' the little blonde sneered. 'What a sloppy house this is! They ought to tear it down and construct a slum on the site.'

She's looking for a fight, Molly warned herself as she struggled out of her mackinaw. And she won't get it from me. Tim wants me to treat her nicely—but not too nicely, of course. 'I *have* had offers,' she said wryly. 'Bettencourt Construction offered me half-a-million just for the site—and offered to move the house for me, if I could find someplace to move it to.'

'And you turned the offer down,' gasped Susan, almost dropping her coffee-mug.

'There wasn't much choice,' Molly sighed. 'You have no idea what land is selling for these days, and I've seven acres up here, right on the edge of the bluffs. But you just try to find a plot available at a reasonable price to which I could have the house moved! Impossible. And I have to live somewhere!'

'But you could live in Paris, New York——'

'Not me,' said Molly. 'I'm a small-town person. Did you get something for breakfast?'

'No. For some reason Aunt Gerda stormed off when I came down. I only asked for croissants, you know, and she blew up as if I'd ordered something out of the ordinary. As far as I can tell, she's upstairs telling that Captain person all about it. And that's another thing, Molly Patterson. How *could* you allow someone like that to spend the night with us? Why, I quivered in my bed all night!'

Why you're a thoroughly disgusting person, Molly assessed to herself as she turned back to the stove. Only Tim was close enough, though, to hear her mutter, 'In *whose* bed?'

'Count to ten,' he murmured in Molly's ear as he helped Moira to shed her outer gear.

'I've done that twice,' she muttered in return. 'Susan, would you like some wheat-cakes? Or more toast? Or a grapefruit? I have a couple of grapefruit in the refrigerator.'

'Nothing.' The blonde seemed to contain more bad temper than could be explained by a simple hangover. After all, it *was* Christmas Day. 'A piece of dry toast,' she ordered. 'Trim the crusts, and please don't burn it!'

Ten, eleven, twelve, Molly counted to herself as she prepared the bread. And no crusts? Well, she has enough crust for both herself *and* the bread. Fifteen, sixteen, seventeen—— She looked down at Moira, standing at her side, fingers busy. Eighteen, nineteen, twenty, the child signed, and grinned up at Molly as she did so.

'You cut that out,' Molly signed back to her. 'She's your mother.'

Moira shook her head from side to side as she signed, 'No! No! Never!'

'And would you two stop that stupid finger exercising,' Susan grumbled. 'Isn't it bad enough that we're snowbound up here in the wilderness, without having that idiot mumbo-jumbo being flashed in our faces?'

'I don't mind,' Tim interjected mildly. 'It's sort of attractive, knowing that they can communicate as well as they can. But why now, Moira?'

The little girl looked up at him with an innocent expression on her face. 'Because the battery in my hearing aid has gone dead,' she said very solemnly. 'So until I get a replacement I'll just have to struggle along with lip-reading and sign language. Would your friends in Paris like to see that, *Mama*?'

There was a gargling sound from the table as Susan almost choked herself to death on her coffee. Tim hurried over and pounded her on the back—which did nothing to help her cause.

That's the first time I've heard her call Susan *Mother*, Molly thought. Does that mean the child is reaching out to her parent? But then look at the gleam in the girl's eyes. It's more as if she called her that as a challenge! And feel the tension! The air is so thick you could cut it with a knife!

Little Bertie, the puppy, took that moment to wander across the kitchen threshold. Moira dropped to her knees and tried to coax him forward. The puppy wagged its tail madly, and began to wobble across the highly polished linoleum floor. Twice his legs slipped out from under him and he landed flat on his belly, with an astonished look on his face. When he scrabbled to his feet he was facing the wrong direction, and his first few steps bounced him off Susan's leg.

'Get that filthy beast away from me!' she screamed. Her foot drew back, and had not Tim's intervening hand caught at her ankle, she would have kicked the little bundle of fur. Moira dived forward across the floor, snatched up her pet, and rolled away from the table.

'Don't you *ever* touch my dog,' the child said threateningly. 'Not ever!'

'Have your fun,' grated Susan. 'Your father has refused all my offers, my lawyer tells me, so I shall go into court in January to get custody. And then we'll see, young lady, about dogs and wild language and rudeness—won't we?'

'No, we won't,' Moira muttered, moving behind her father for protection. 'No, we won't neither. I'd druther run away than live with you, you—Daddy, tell her!'

'Yes, perhaps I must,' Tim responded softly. He looked over the heads of the pair close to him, straight into Molly's eyes. From long practice she could read his hurt, his pleading, and she knew he was about to pose a whopper of a statement. 'There won't be any question about custody, Susan,' he continued. 'In case you didn't read your mail several years ago, I not only have a custody award from the French court, but I also have an adoption award from an English court. I'm sure you wouldn't want to have to explain an American court about blood-tests and things like that, would you? Especially with Mr

DeMoins as your lawyer?'

'You devil,' muttered Susan as she scraped her chair back. 'You damn devil! Maybe I will anyway, just to prove—and maybe I'll tell your darling little Moira all about it too. How would you like that, to be held up as a bachelor non-father?'

Tim's face turned chillingly cold. Susan backed away from him, her hand over her mouth as if to block the words that could not be recalled.

'Go ahead,' he said softly. 'Moira and I have talked at great length about this. She knows everything there is to know, except for an actual name. I'm sure you'd be happy to have all that splashed over the front pages of the *Globe*? And I mean—everything, Susan.' He stopped talking for just a moment, and a slow smile spread across his face. 'And while we're at it, I want you to be the first to know that Molly and I are getting married!'

His ex-wife backed up a couple more steps, until she was against the wall. She nibbled nervously at her fist, fire in her eyes. 'You think you've won everything, don't you,' she muttered. 'You and Miss Goody Two-Shoes there. Well, I could tell *her* a thing or two, believe me! I'm not finished with you, Tim Holland, not by a long shot!' At which she turned and ran from the room.

'Well,' Moira drawled, 'isn't life full of surprises! Is that true, Dad, that you and Aunt Molly are going to——'

'Maybe I spoke a little prematurely,' he told the child. 'Why don't you go play with your puppy while your aunt and I have a long talk?'

'Yes, why don't you do that?' Molly seconded grimly. Her mind was in a whirl of confusion. Everything she had ever wanted was within her grasp, and to her surprise she wasn't quite sure she wanted it. Not this way, like a sudden announcement from on high, with no explanation,

no solicitation. As if Molly Patterson had nothing better
to do than hang around until Tim Holland should—damn
the tears!

'Molly, I'm sorry to break it to you that way.' Tim
moved to her side and put a hand on her shoulder. She
shook it off. A very concerned young man took one step
backwards. 'Molly? It's something I had to do. Susan
knows she hasn't a chance in court if I'm engaged to be
married to you. No judge on the North Shore would
consider *her* over *you*. Molly?'

'I don't want to talk to you right now,' she told him
bitterly, turning her back. 'I've lots of work to do—and I
just don't want to talk to you, Tim Holland. Go
away—please!'

'All right.' She heard the footsteps retreating, the sound
of the kitchen door closing, and then she went at the
dishes, at the supper plans, at almost anything she could
find to do, just to keep her hands busy.

As the day passed things returned to normal, but Molly
felt walled away from everything and everybody. Aunt
Gerda came down to help with the meal preparation. She
had a great deal to say, but it all sounded as if she were
on the other side of a wall. Moira bounced in and out, and
almost penetrated the shield, but even the child knew
something was wrong, and made no attempt to push.
Captain Francis wandered in, received a quiet signal from
Gerda, and announced that he 'had better get out and do
some shovelling.'

Tim was already outside, shovel in hand. He had
expanded the path out of the back door eastward to the
barn, and had cleared enough space so that the doors
could be swung open. He stopped long enough to have
lunch, eaten in complete silence in the kitchen, then
started on a path from the front door to the look-out point

on the bluffs.

'That's pretty silly,' Aunt Gerda insisted as she came out for a momentary breath of air. 'Who the devil wants to walk out there?'

'Nobody, I suppose,' Tim replied glumly. 'It's just something that Molly's father always did—he was in love with the sea, and always wanted access to the point. So to me it's habit. And it won't hurt anybody, will it?'

'I don't suppose so,' said Gerda. 'Only we'd be better off if we had a path down to the road.'

'That comes next,' he sighed, grounding his shovel. 'But I don't think the road will be passable until it's ploughed again, and that won't happen for another couple of days. What does the radio say?'

'Just that,' Gerda informed him. 'They look for the skies to clear tonight or tomorrow, the DPW crews are out ploughing the main streets at the moment, they expect to get to Magnolia in a couple of days, and don't go out on the roads unless you have to. And we don't have to!'

'The devil we don't,' Tim said angrily. 'Another two days penned up in a house with *that* pair? God knows what they'll think of. The only sure thing is that they'll try *something*.'

'Well, you really blew it, I hear. How is it that a man as smart as you can act so stupidly, nephew?'

'Just practice, I suppose. If I could add up all the times I've really screwed things up where Molly is concerned—but I honestly thought she'd be willing to go along with an engagement to help me with Moira.'

'Yes,' his aunt commented sarcastically. 'And I heard that's just the way you put it, right? Or wasn't there something about "and, Susan, you'll be the first to know that Molly and I are to be married"?'

'I—seem to remember words like that,' he said

cautiously.

'And she was, wasn't she? Susan? She was the first to know?'

'I—go ahead, twist the knife,' he snapped. 'So I had my foot in my mouth again, didn't I? Yes, it's all true. I should have told Molly first—asked Molly first. But it did seem like a fine time to go so cautiously with Molly that I don't seem to be going anywhere at all! What do I do now?'

'You ask me?' His aunt dismissed him with a shrug of her shoulders. 'I never knew a man to have so much trouble getting a girl who already loves him to marry him! Never!'

'You really believe that?'

'Of course I believe it. Molly Patterson has been in love with you for a hundred years or more. Now if we can only keep you out of the way while I try to patch things up—why don't you go ahead and dig that other path down to the road? And when you're done with that, how about a scenic walk along the cliffs, or maybe you could start on the road? It's only two miles from here to the intersection, right?'

'Boy, you really know how to make a guy feel wanted,' he grumbled.

'Tell me about it,' his aunt told him as she turned and went back to the house.

Inside, still busy as a bee, Molly had arrived at the point where tears stopped flowing because there was no liquid left to flow. The fact that her brain was no longer working hardly seemed important. When Gerda bustled in, cheeks red with the cold, Molly paid no attention, but went on with her unnecessary tasks.

But when her adopted aunt began to rattle pans and

make a commotion in the work-areas which Molly had just polished, she did essay a small protest. 'Well, I can't help that,' Aunt Gerda insisted. 'Tomorrow is Tim's birthday, and he *has* to have a cake.'

'He *is* a cake,' muttered Molly. 'You're making——?'

'Strawberry shortcake,' Gerda interrupted. 'His favourite. With the old New England recipe, and plenty of whipped cream——'

'All I have is the canned whip,' said Molly. 'Whipped cream, strawberries—do you know what I'd like to do with——'

'No,' Gerda interrupted again. 'And I'd rather you didn't tell me. Why don't you go give Moira a language lesson, or go upstairs and mope in your own room?'

'Maybe I should go out and help Tim shovel snow,' Molly offered tentatively.

'No, that's a terrible idea, love. Leave him alone to his misery.'

'*His* misery? He should catch cold and die from *his* misery,' Molly snapped. 'Do you know what that nephew of yours said to me?'

'No, I don't think I do, and I'm too busy to listen,' the older woman said. 'Get out of my kitchen.'

'*My* kitchen,' Molly returned, but her heart wasn't in the argument. Obviously Gerda rated Tim's birthday cake higher than Molly's peace of mind. She fiddled with her apron for a moment, then gave up and stalked out into the living-room where Moira was busy with a colouring book and crayons.

'Christmas Day is always tough,' Molly commented, sinking into an armchair.

'I hadn't noticed,' the little girl said. 'I've had such a good time that—lordy, Aunt Molly, I've never had such a nice day in all my life! Not ever!'

Surprised that someone could be cheerful on such a terrible day, Molly turned on her side to examine the little face. It was alight from an inner glow, there was no doubt about that. 'Presents?' she probed.

'Oh, they were nice,' Moira answered, 'but there's so much more to Christmas than presents, isn't there? There's so much lovin' and things like that—and then you and Daddy are going to get married—and what more could a girl ask?'

'That—really isn't all that important—your dad and I are getting married, is it?'

Moira squirmed around and gave her a startled look. 'Not that important? That's crazy! It's the very most important thing of the whole day, that's what!' Her little hand stole across the space separating them and caught up Molly's.

'I didn't realise,' Molly whispered.

'Well—it is,' the child reported.

Molly took a grip on herself; shook herself by the imagination, reorganised her priorities, re-established goals, all in a fraction of a second, then returned to the fray a little more lighthearted. 'For a girl with no battery in her hearing aid, you hear pretty good,' she commented drily.

'Pretty well,' Moira corrected. 'You got lousy grammar. Did Sister Alice really teach you?'

'Yes, she did. What about the battery?'

'There's nothing wrong with my battery,' the child announced in a very self-satisfied tone. 'It must have been a loose connection or something. Every time that—that woman comes near me my battery seems to go on the blink.'

'Yes, I can see that,' her aunt declared. 'Or something. Where's your dog?'

'Well, they were tired from getting up so early, so Shag went into my room to rest, and Bertie went along with him, and I thought that was a good idea. I shut the door so that—woman—couldn't get at them.'

'That's a nice idea.'

'When are you two going to get married—and can I be in the wedding?' Moira wanted to know.

'I—don't think your father is quite ready for a wedding,' Molly answered. 'First there has to be an engagement period, you know. A time when we have a chance to think things over.' Molly took a quick peep to see how that line of argument was going. Moira had indeed got up too early. Her eyes were blinking steadily, and as Molly watched, both eyelids came down and stayed there. 'And I don't think I'm going to marry your father,' Molly whispered. 'Although I may kill him.'

'That's nice,' Moira mumbled.

Molly watched for a moment; the child was completely out. And how long has it been since I could do that? Molly asked herself. Fall asleep on a hardwood floor; have so much confidence in my elders that all they had to say was taken with complete trust? How long has it taken me to become a sceptical spinster? Ten years—fifteen? Why is it that every time I think the world is looking better, Tim Holland can come along and upset my applecart? Well, he won't get away with it this time. I don't know how I'm going to do it, but I have a revenge list a mile long, and I mean to get even with all of them. Susan Holland, for stealing my man, Alfred DeMoins, for almost stealing my—well, enough said about that. And Tim Holland, for—for letting me love him all those years under false pretences. There's only one restriction. When I get even with Tim, it must be in such a manner that Moira doesn't suffer as well!

From behind the closed kitchen door she heard a murmur of voices. Captain Francis had reappeared, and he and Aunt Gerda were talking. And that's a strange pair, Molly smiled to herself. Whoever would have thought, at their age! Love must be wonderful, when it comes from both sides. But there now. If the Captain is downstairs, maybe I could hustle up and get a couple of the bedrooms straightened out!

The word was mother to the deed. Alfred and Susan were still not accounted for, so she stole up the stairs in stockinged feet and began to work in the Captain's room. The big wide bed was a terrible mess. Molly grinned as she replaced the sheets from the hall closet, made everything up as pretty as could be, straightened and picked up, and was still smiling as she stepped out into the corridor.

Gerda's room needed hardly a lick and a promise. The bed was as unused as it had been before the holidays. Molly was laughing as she came out into the corridor and ran smack into Alfred.

'Well, what have we here?' he said, in that oily voice that sent shivers up her spine.

'What we have here is the ordinary garden-variety room maid,' she told him. 'And if you would kindly get out of my way I could get about it.'

'Now, now, Molly,' he said, reaching out both arms in her direction. 'Everyone seems to be busy——'

'Except for Susan,' Molly interrupted. 'And if you think I add two and two and can't get four, you're sadly mistaken, Mr DeMoins.'

'Mr DeMoins? My, how formal we've become! It wasn't like this the last time we met. Besides, Susan is fast asleep—the strain, you understand. All her problems. Of which you are but one, Moll. Why don't we sneak into your bedroom and see if we can't take up where we left off all those weeks ago?'

'I don't sneak into bedrooms,' she snarled at him, more furious than she had been in years. Sweet Molly Patterson, she thought, the girl who wouldn't hurt a flea. And here I am ready to kill this man!

Unfortunately, while she was thinking he was moving. With the skill of much practice, he trapped her, bundled her down the hall to her own room, and opened the door. 'Inside, love,' he laughed softly.

'I'll scream,' she threatened.

'Now, now,' he teased, but she could hear the iron behind the soft words. Here's a man with rape on his mind, she told herself as she let him push her into the room. He followed close behind, keeping her wrapped up in his arms, until he stumbled over Shag's recumbent form. The old dog stirred, waddled to his feet, and took a good look at the couple. Alfred, not sure of himself in the face of the gargantuan animal, stepped back half a pace. And there, Molly told herself dispassionately, is the opening. Her mind running cold and clear and totally unexcited, she moved in his direction. His hands came up again, reaching for her shoulders. Thankful that she was wearing slacks instead of a dress, Molly waited until he had reached optimum range, then slammed her knee viciously up into his groin.

Everything happened in just the way her instructor at the martial arts class had explained. Alfred seemed to draw in a shrieking breath, clutched madly at himself, and collapsed on the floor, his feet kicking in agony. Shag came over to watch, neither pleased nor angry—as befitting a dog who has known dozens of crazy humans. The thud and the groans must have carried down the stairs. Feet pounded, and Captain Francis crashed through the door, ready for almost anything.

'Did I kill him?' Molly asked hopefully.

'No, but you surely put a dent in his future prospects for heirs,' the Captain chuckled as he made a cursory examination. 'Say something impolite, did he? He'll be out of action for a long time. It was an accident, no doubt?'

'I don't think so,' Molly said solemnly. 'That's number one.'

Shag, deciding finally which side he was on, moved up to Alfred's perspiring forehead and began to lick with that huge rough tongue of his. The Captain, obviously an unrepentant sinner on his own, asked no further questions. 'He'll need ice-cubes,' he mused.

'Ice-cubes?' queried Molly in surprise.

'Well, I don't think a couple of Band-aids will do him any good,' the Captain chuckled as he took her arm, helped her step over Alfred's recumbent form, and led her out of the room.

CHAPTER NINE

MORNING, December the twenty-sixth. It *had* to be morning; all the clocks said so, even though the sun had failed to make an appearance. The snow had ceased, but leaden clouds reigned from horizon to horizon. All the lights were on at Logan International Airport to her west, and the towers of Boston sparkled in the distance. Molly took a deep breath of the damp cold air and gave thanks for the path which Tim had shovelled to no purpose. From her vantage point on the observation platform in the gazebo, no matter which way she looked, the world was mantled in white. Soberly she walked back to the house and into the kitchen.

'We have enough fuel for the generator for another twenty-four hours,' she announced as she bent to pry off her boots.

'Well, thank God for that,' Gerda returned. 'Now are you ready for breakfast?'

'Yes, I'm ready. No sign of our other—people?'

'Moira's up and about. The Captain is shaving. Mr DeMoins, I'm given to understand, isn't feeling well and won't be down.'

'And Susan?'

'You said *people*,' Aunt Gerda grumbled. 'I don't consider Susan to be in that category—good morning, Tim.'

'Good morning,' he groaned as he limped in from the hall. Molly took a deep breath to settle her nerves. Just the seeing of him was bothering her these days. Not as

155

handsome as usual, he looked just a little frayed around the edges, and was not quite standing straight.

'I ache,' he announced grandly.

'All that stupid snow-shovelling yesterday,' his aunt told him, without the slightest bit of sympathy in her voice. 'Here are your sausages, Molly dear.'

Molly dear did her best to hide the grin as she settled into a chair and admired her breakfast. Sausages, scrambled eggs, toast, coffee, orange juice. Typically American. And dear Tim—still grumbling as he tried to fit himself into the chair opposite. Getting even with people like Tim was difficult; things seemed to slide off his back without leaving a mark. Slide off his back!

'After I finish my breakfast I know just the thing to make you feel better,' she said innocently. Perhaps too innocently? He's staring at me as if he were the cobra and I the mongoose!

'How kind of you, Miss Patterson,' he replied cautiously. 'Perhaps you could tell me how I am to be done good to?'

'Your syntax leaves a little something to be desired,' she chuckled. 'I'm going to massage your back——'

'Why do I get the feeling I won't like this?' he interrupted. 'With what?'

'Why, eucalyptus oil, of course. My mother swore by it for backaches!'

'The very thing,' Aunt Gerda contributed.

'Not on your life!' Tim managed to work up enough energy to protest, but the two women paid him no attention. 'I don't intend to become a human stink-pile,' he added.

'There's nothing wrong with eucalyptus,' Molly said firmly a few minutes later as she bullied him into lying down on the sofa in the living-room, an old towel beneath him. 'According to the *Geographic*, koalas eat nothing but eucalyptus leaf. Don't wriggle so!' With practised skill her fingers dug into his tortured muscles.

'That feels good,' he murmured. 'I *really* thought you planned to murder or maim me.'

'That comes tomorrow,' she promised, applying more power to her seeking fingers.

'And you'll smell of eucalyptus for days,' he chuckled. 'Didn't you know that koalas are famous for bad breath? That oil is so penetrating that you'll be days trying to wash if off!'

'Not me,' Molly told him. 'You may—you probably will, Tim Holland, but I'm wearing rubber gloves!'

'What in the world is that awful smell!' Susan appeared at the living-room door then walked in. 'Timmy? How could you stand—what is that woman doing to you?'

'You needn't worry, Susan,' he said cheerfully. 'Anyone willing to marry me is authorised to use whatever rubbing oil she wants. Eucalyptus oil. I'm thinking of importing it from Australia!'

'That's nonsense,' his former wife sniffed. 'Alfred wants to talk to you, Timmy. He has an idea——'

'But maybe I don't want to talk to him,' Tim stated flatly. 'I understand that he's—incapacitated.' He rolled over and sat up, the better to watch Susan's face. 'Captain Francis told me all about his little escapade. And when he gets well enough to have visitors, I'm going to pound him to a pulp.'

'You don't have to become so damn macho,' Susan snapped. 'I want to get out of this rats' nest as fast as I can, but I'm——'

'Why, you wouldn't want to rush off and miss my birthday party?' Tim, at his sarcastic best, was almost believable. To everyone except Molly, who knew him better than he knew himself. He's really angry, she thought. Boiling underneath. If Susan and her Alfred don't watch out, they're going to get badly burned!

'Oh—well,' Susan stammered, 'I guess we wouldn't do that——'

'And besides,' he continued inexorably, 'your lawyer's car is under an eight-foot snowdrift. Why don't you get him out of bed so he can start shovelling?'

'Tim,' Susan said, exasperated, 'it doesn't have to end like this. Regardless of how you feel now, we *did* have something going for us. Talk to Alfred, please.' It was the sort of appeal that Tim could understand.

'All right,' he sighed, 'I'll talk to your lawyer, Susan, but I can't promise you anything. My mind is pretty well locked in concrete. Is lover-boy awake?'

'He's still in bed,' Susan replied, 'but he's able to talk. I told him I'd ask you to go right up.'

'I'll need a few minutes,' said Tim as he stretched to get up from the sofa. The low coffee-table was between him and his former wife, and Molly had just set the opened bottle of oil down on it. But Susan, filled with a sudden exultation, crowded against the table and tried to throw her arms around Tim's neck.

'Watch out for the oil!' Molly and Tim both shouted at the same time. Susan looked down to see the bottle tottering, and grabbed at it, but a moment too late. Instead of getting both hands around the neck of the bottle, the little blonde managed to get both hands into the flow of oil spilling out over the table. Molly, her hands swathed in the rubber gloves, snatched the bottle out of the way, but not before the other woman's hands were soaked by the aromatic mixture. Tim snatched up the towel on which he had been lying, and managed to sop up the oil before it ran off the coffee table on to the rug.

'Damn! Damn! Damn!' With tears in her eyes, Susan stood helplessly in the middle of the room, with both hands elevated to eye-level.

'Here.' Molly offered the use of her apron.

'My best clothes,' Susan muttered. 'God, everything I touch in this house turns to manure! It's all your fault, Molly Patterson! I think you do it all on purpose! Damn you!'

'Now you know better than that.' Tim came around the coffee-table and tried to help in the drying-up. 'It was all an accident. Now, if you want me to talk to that—to your lawyer, you'd better go wash your hands and come with me.'

The enticement was strong enough to shut off the tears, but as Tim escorted Susan out of the room she looked back over her shoulder and gave Molly a glare that the Medusa would have cherished.

'Why, she hates me,' Molly murmured as the pair of them disappeared. 'She really *hates* me! *She's* had all the good life, but she——' For a home-body like Molly, who had never really felt a measure of pure hatred before, it was a startling revelation.

'Who hates you?' Moira bubbled into the room, her face covered with chocolate and her arms full of puppy.

'Good lord,' Molly exclaimed. 'What are you? An accident looking for a place to happen?'

'I was just helping out,' Moira said defensively. 'Auntie Gerda is making the strawberry shortcake, and a dozen cupcakes as well.'

'Chocolate cupcakes?' Molly tried to suppress the grin, but had no luck at it. Moira's puppy was squirming around in the child's arms, trying to lick off some of the excess around her mouth.

'Who hates you?' the child asked again.

'Oh—nobody, I suppose. It was all a misunderstanding.' Yes, Molly told herself as she watched the two in front of her enjoying each other. I've never had anyone who *hated* me before. What a terrifying experience it is to discover that my very own cousin hates me! I wonder how long, and why?

'Oh, I forgot,' Moira interrupted her thoughts. 'Auntie Gerda says if you're going to make the supper you'll have to get busy pretty quick, because there's only Cornish game hen left, and somebody has to stuff them all and like that——'

'I get the picture,' Molly chuckled. 'And in the meantime, young lady, I want you to put your puppy down in his box over there while you scoot upstairs and get a real bath. Cleanliness is next to godliness.'

'Good lord, where do you get all those *ucky* sayings?' Moira queried.

'Get lost, or I'll *ucky* you,' Molly threatened as she made her way out to the kitchen.

The two women in the kitchen were going all out on an international dinner for Tim's birthday celebration. Stuffed Cornish rock hen, asparagus flown in from Mexico, Idaho potatoes, *petits pois* from California, and a chocolate mousse—the latter Moira's choice as she wandered through the kitchen at one o'clock, looking for her puppy.

'He's probably just wandering,' Aunt Gerda told the worried child. 'Look for Shag. They're always together.' Molly kept one eye on the girl for a moment. The puppy's disappearance was but one of several odd interruptions. Tim had appeared at eleven-thirty, shaking his head as he snatched up a cup of coffee.

'They want the world,' he reported dismally. 'I got so

mad I told them both I wouldn't give them another cent. Not a damn penny. And that damn DeMoins! Imagine the nerve of the man! He said something wild about you, Molly, and I was forced to make him eat his words.'

'Oh, Tim,' the peace-loving Molly chided. And then, 'Did you hurt your knuckles?'

'All in a good cause,' he answered cheerily, rubbing his right hand gently. 'You and I have to talk, Molly.'

'Talking won't stuff the chicken,' she told him.

He shook his head dolefully. 'I'll be in the den,' he said. 'Paperwork, you know.'

'I just don't understand him any more,' Molly told Gerda. 'Sometimes he's good, and sometimes he's—bad, and——'

'And when he's bad he's very, very bad,' Gerda chuckled. 'Where the devil is the poison princess going?' She gestured out of the kitchen window. Susan, dressed in her high-fashion clothing, and obviously shivering in the cold, was out probing around Alfred's big Cadillac.

'She'll never get that car out of the drifts,' Molly commented. A few moments later Susan came storming through the kitchen, using a great many four-letter words—some of which Molly had never heard before.

'Very impressive vocabulary,' Aunt Gerda said drily as the kitchen door slammed. Moira appeared again, crestfallen.

'I still can't find Bertie,' the child reported. 'Is there another chocolate cupcake?'

'Lunch is in twenty minutes,' Molly cautioned. 'Rouse Shag. He'll help you.'

'Well, I dunno,' sighed Moira. 'Shag's such a lot of dog it's hard to wake him up.'

'You'll never know until you try,' Molly chided, and promptly burned her finger on the oven door. So what with one thing and another time passed, it was two o'clock, the luncheon table was set, and a general call went out. Susan came, looking daggers at the world. Alfred declined; it seemed he had some problem with his mouth. Captain Francis came in like a hurricane; Timmy drifted along a moment later.

'And where's Moira?' Heads around the table turned.

'The last I heard she was looking for Bertie,' Molly reported.

'The pup is missing?' asked Tim. Yes, the pup is missing, Molly lectured herself. And the girl was worried. Why the devil couldn't I stop what I was doing and help? There's a lot more to living than getting the right stuffing for rock hen!

'I—think we'd better have a look around the house,' she suggested. 'Those cellar stairs are a problem, and I'm not sure I locked the door this morning.'

'I'll check the cellar,' Tim said, suddenly serious. 'Captain?'

'Let me scoot around upstairs,' the older man proposed.

'Susan? You can check the downstairs rooms.'

'Not me,' Susan muttered. 'I'm here for lunch, not for a house-to-house search.'

'I'll do it,' Aunt Gerda volunteered bitterly. 'I don't feel like eating next to somebody like you, Susan Holland. I hope you plan to drop your married name soon. It's a drain on my Christian sensibilities.'

What Susan had to say in return went unheard as the search party set out, leaving Molly alone with Susan. A restless, worried Molly, and a stolid Susan, chewing at her food like a robot.

'I've got a funny feeling,' Molly said quietly.

'That's not all you've got that's funny!' Susan snarled.

'I intend to get out of this house as soon as I can, Molly Patterson. And I don't intend to come back ever. Sweet little nauseating Molly! God, how sick you've made me feel. Did it hurt when I stole Tim out from under your nose? If I hadn't found Europe so great I would have loved to be here to watch you squirm after the wedding.'

'I'm sorry you feel that way,' Molly told her cousin, 'but right at the moment—did you hear that?'

'Hear what? All I've heard lately is the damn house rattling. When is it going to fall down?'

Molly shook her head in disgust. 'You really are a rotten person, aren't you, Susan!' And at that moment she heard the noise again—from outside. Panic edged up into her throat. Without thinking she grabbed up her boots, stuffed her feet into them, and went dashing out into the snow without a coat. Clear of the house and all its miscellaneous sounds, it became easier to spot the source of her worries. From far beyond the house, over by the bluff, Shag was whining, scratching at something on the ground.

'Oh lord!' Molly screamed, and started running. Slaloming might have been a better term for it, as, with knees pulled high, she cut a path around the house in the direction of the path dug towards the observation platform. Shag, hearing her come, began to bark. The old animal came down the path a few paces, barked again, and turned back. Without her glasses, Molly could hardly see what the trouble was, but there seemed to be a bundle lying on the ground just at the edge of the bluff. She kept her legs pumping, but a slight glaze that had formed over the snow made it slippery going. From behind her she could hear the sounds of pursuit.

The observation platform had been cleared clean down to the wood. When her foot hit the platform Molly's foot slipped and she went crashing down. At this close a range she could see that the bundle already there was Moira. The little girl had obviously slipped, knocked off her hat against one of the wooden stanchions, and slashed a cut across her forehead. Her eyes were closed, her legs were extended below the railing out into empty air, but in her arms was the struggling Bertie.

'Oh, God, sweetheart,' Molly muttered as she fumbled herself to a sitting position and tugged the child's head into her lap. 'Moira, love! Moira!'

The child moaned, but did not move. Fighting down her anxiety, Molly made a quick check. Arms and legs seemed solid; only the child's head, where she had smashed into the pole, showed evidence of damage. And then Tim was there.

'You forgot your coat,' he growled as he dropped the heavy mackinaw on Molly's shoulders and reached down to take charge of his daughter. Molly, pushed back out of the way, struggled into the coat, all the while watching while Tim checked his daughter in almost a professional manner.

'Take the pup,' he instructed her. Molly grabbed at the struggling bundle of fur and clutched it tightly up under her chin. Tim stood, picking Moira up with him. 'Hospital,' he commanded. 'A concussion, perhaps.'

'My truck,' Molly said tersely. 'Four-wheel drive. I'll drive. I can handle it better.'

'You're probably right,' he told her as he padded down the slippery path and began to cut across towards the barn. 'But since it's going to be a murderous drive, and I'm the one with all the muscles, we'll do it my way.' Molly was almost ready to object, when the common sense of it all intervened. Of course he was the stronger. And more experienced. And wasn't it just a taste of wonder to have a man take charge like that?

With his long legs he gradually pulled away from her, making protest academic. In the clear cold of winter something teased at Molly's nostrils. Tim, of course, smelled to high heaven of eucalyptus oil. But now he was far enough away from her, and her nose was still being bothered by that overwhelming smell. She slowed for a moment and sniffed again. From the puppy, no less. Little Bertie smelled as if he had had liberal contact with Australia's strongest export!

Tim needed help with the barn door by that time. In his spurt of shovelling the previous day he had cleared a path for the door to swing out, and dug a couple of ruts down to the road. But the old doors were heavy, and with his daughter still in his arms, he was handicapped.

Molly bent to release the pup in a cleared space, and set her shoulder to the door. At about that moment Captain Francis came puffing up from the house and added his weight. The doors groaned, but swung clear.

'The lawyer,' Tim called. 'Get him out here. We'll take him to the hospital too. Tell him he's got two minutes!' The Captain started back to the house to pass the word. Molly swung around the far side of the Bronco, climbed up into the high seat, and fished for the emergency keys, held by a magnet to the underside of the driver's seat. Tim moved in beside her and took over. The motor was reluctant to start, but once coaxed it burst into a roar of power. Molly moved into the back seat and took Moira's head in her lap.

'I'll take it easy,' Tim advised. 'Let me know if there's any change in her breathing. I think she's just knocked out, but we can't be too careful. What damn foolishness took her running out into the snow like that?'

Before Molly could think of an answer Alfred was at

the car, protesting all the way. 'I can't leave all my—luggage,' the lawyer complained. 'And it's dangerous riding in this kind of weather.'

'Shut up and get in,' Tim commanded coldly. 'You're doubly a fool if you think I'm going to leave a skunk like you back here.' The lawyer took one look at him, and complied.

'We'll try the Addison,' Molly called out of the back window at Captain Francis, who nodded and waved an arm, then ducked out of the way as Tim backed the truck out of the garage, wheeled it around in the cleared area, shifted into four-wheel drive, and took them bumpily down the track that led to the road.

The little truck ploughed along, slipping and sliding from side to side, groaning over each hillock of snow, but never actually stopping. When it vaulted over the ridge piled up by the snowploughs it almost seemed that it was blowing its heart away, but the four-wheel drive and Tim's skilled handling sustained it. They dropped with a mighty clangour into the middle of the street, where the earlier ploughing had partially cleared the way.

'I don't think I want to go,' Alfred complained.

'I think you do,' Tim snarled at him. 'We might get stuck along the way, and you're a prime candidate to help push us out. In the meantime, shut up and save your breath!'

They rolled down the narrow access road at something like four miles an hour, the truck swaying from side to side, and bouncing up and down front to back. 'Worse than that lobster boat you were going to make our fortune with,' Molly called to Tim. 'Remember? The one that sank just off Normans Woe when you were sixteen?'

'It was a good idea,' he replied. 'I was just unlucky. That's been the story of my life, Molly Patterson. What road shall we take?'

'I wouldn't dare go through the village,' she called back at him. 'That's Route 127 up ahead, Western Avenue. Why don't you give it a try?'

Tim leaned forward and peered out through the windscreen. 'It looks as if they've tried to plough it,' he agreed. 'As usual, we're in God's hands, love.'

That had such a nice sound to it that Molly travelled the next two miles cushioned above the seat by some force—some power, that sustained her against all attacks. It must have been all mental, for as far as she could note out of the corner of her eyes, Alfred was showing definite signs of seasickness. And the shifting and rocking and swaying as the little truck battled the snow was making a terrible mess out of the cabin of the vehicle. Still, with a strength she did not know she had, she held Moira's comatose body against her, held her breath as Tim was called upon for more skill than she had expected, and managed to survive until they reached the bridge where Western Avenue passed over the Blynmon Canal. There, to her absolute joy, two ploughs were moving eastward ahead of them in tandem, clearing the roadway, sending plumes of snow high in the air towards either side. And Moira stirred in her arms and opened her eyes.

'Thank you, God,' Molly whispered as they came up to the Clifford Avenue turn-off, where Tim regretfully saluted the ploughs and turned north. 'Just a few blocks,' he announced in as calm a voice as he could muster.

'Moira's holding on,' she reassured him. 'Go carefully.'

Her comment brought him back to his senses. He lifted his foot slightly off the accelerator and let the vehicle slow down. Clifford had been cleaned, a surprise in itself, and when they came to the corner where Emerson branched left he took it cautiously, and made the two short blocks that brought them into the entrance to the emergency room at the Addison-Gilbert Hospital. When she climbed down from the high cab on trembling legs she took a deep breath and laid a hand on Tim's arm.

'I'll say one thing for it,' she confessed, 'I never could have made it myself, Tim.' He smiled at her as he lifted his daughter out of the back seat.

'And knowing how much that kind of admission costs you, Moll,' he chuckled, 'I'll treasure that statement forever and ever.'

'Alfred,' Molly said in her most exasperated voice, 'I really don't care *what* you do.' The pair of them were in the lounge of the hospital, waiting. Tim, as a father might, had gone through the emergency procedures with his daughter, and Molly had no room for anything except her anxieties. It had been almost two hours since their arrival, and so far she had heard not a word. Alfred, after a brief patchwork exam in the emergency room, had been turned loose to go where he would.

'I saw a couple of cabs moving,' she suggested to the worried lawyer. 'Why don't you call one of them, and go over to the Cape Ann Motor Inn. I'm sure they'd make room for you. Or the alternative, why don't you let a doctor admit you to the hospital? You don't exactly look healthy, you know.'

'If I don't it's all your fault,' he whined. 'All your fault.'

'Probably,' she retorted, not the least bit like the old sympathetic Molly Patterson. 'And I'd do it again if the occasion warranted!'

He backed away from her, both hands up in front of himself, protectively. 'What in the world did I ever see in you anyway?' she asked rhetorically. 'Or Susan. What in the world did Susan ever see in you? You don't have the backbone of a jellyfish! Maybe what I need now is to give you a knuckle sandwich.' She balled up her fist and whacked it into the palm of her other hand as she took a couple of steps in Alfred's direction.

'You can't do that,' he blustered. 'You might hurt me!'

'Yes,' she agreed, 'but think how nice that would make me feel, Alfred!' Two more steps and Alfred struck his colours. No arguments from him about the weaker sex; not after that wild ride through the snow. No sooner did her foot hit the ground than he turned and fled through the double doors.

So Molly was laughing when Tim came through those same doors a moment or two later, a surprised look on his face. 'Something funny?' he asked.

'Not really,' she sighed. 'Lack of the true Christian impulse. I was picking on a lesser mortal. How's Moira?'

'Moira's all right—the doctor thinks,' he assured her. 'But she won't tell me anything about what happened. She wants *you*!'

Tim was silent as he hurried her down the hall and into a cubicle. Dr Hanscomb was standing by the curtained door. 'Why, Molly,' the doctor smiled, 'I didn't know you were married. The little yike says she won't talk to anyone except her mother.'

'*Pro tempore*,' she said solemnly, using up exactly one half of all her Latin education. The doctor grinned and stepped aside. His own Latin was limited to prescription-writing these days.

Moira was lying on a plain examination couch, covered by a sheet. Molly stopped at the entrance and wiped the fog off her glasses and took a good look. The child might not be Tim's natural child, but her little narrow face was firmly set, just the way Tim's had been once when he was on one of his stubborn streaks. When the child saw Molly she sat up on the table and began to cry.

Weeping herself, Molly hurried over and wrapped her arms around the little girl. 'There now,' she comforted, but her words had no effect. Moira, in all the confusion, had lost her hearing aid, and with her head firmly buried in Molly's shoulder she was cut off from communication. Body language was left. Molly hugged her tightly, used one hand to smooth down the hair at the nape of the child's neck, patted her gently in the middle of her back, and waited until the outburst was over. When Moira drew back slightly, far enough to read her lips, she mouthed the words, 'What happened?'

'I don't want Daddy to hear,' the little girl repeated in the same mode as she held up her hands. 'She stole my dog,' Moira signed slowly. 'Took my dog outside and dumped him in the garbage can at the bluff. She isn't real. Nobody could act as mean as that. She *can't* be my mother, can she?'

Molly looked down at the pleading tear-stained cheeks, gave about a tenth of a second to logic and pain and history and Tim, and made up her mind. 'No, of course not,' she signed back. 'How could she be when *I'm* your mother!' The pair of them stared at each other, then broke out into big smiles.

'Well, that's better,' said Dr Hanscomb as he pushed in past the curtain. 'What's been going on, Tim?'

'How would I know?' Tim responded. 'It's some kind of hen party, and evidently mere men are not to know! What's the damage report?'

'The X-rays are clear,' the doctor said. 'No sign of a fracture. Her eyes are clear. There's always a chance of a slight concussion, but that's something only time can tell.

Look, I hear that they're ploughing Route 127 now. Why don't you take the little lady home and put her to bed? Keep her there for twenty-four hours. If she shows any signs of pain or dizziness——'

'I know,' Tim sighed. 'You ex-Army doctors are all the same. Take two aspirins and call you in the morning, right?'

'You needn't get huffy about it,' the doctor chuckled. 'I've been here since Christmas Eve!'

'Do I go home now?' Moira was already halfway off the couch when the doctor put out a restraining arm.

'Not yet,' he laughed. 'You can't come into hospital without having something to show for it all, can you? Now let me disinfect those scratches on your cheek, and we'll add a little bandage—like so. There now, isn't that better?'

The attending nurse held up a little hand mirror. Moira checked herself out, then looked questioningly at Molly. 'It looks very—professional,' Molly responded. 'Very—patientish.'

'There's no such word.' Her newly acquired daughter, showing typical childhood disgust at the limited vocabulary of adults, slid off on to the floor and proceeded to hug her new mother. 'Now I'm ready to go home,' she announced.

There was another little argument at the door. 'Nobody goes to the door except in a wheelchair,' the nurse insisted. 'It's the rule. And I have to drive you by the admissions desk to see if everything is—well, you know—about the bill and all.'

Which resulted in another fifteen-minute delay before they were back in the Bronco again. 'And I'll drive us back,' Tim insisted. It was Molly's car, and practically Molly's road—since she used to drive it every day—and she was about to make a protest when she was smitten with an attack of common sense. After all, he *was* a very attractive male, with a very sensitive ego, who had already told her she was going to marry him. She was still perturbed about that *told her* business, but out in a little truck with snow up to her—well, at least that high—why give him a chance to change his mind?

The drive home was easier and sweeter than the drive to the hospital. The three of them shared the front seat, Tim with both hands on the wheel, Molly with one arm around Moira. The little girl was in some strange shape. Every now and again she would shiver; a moment later she would be laughing. Confused, Molly just hung on.

The doctor was only partly right. The pair of snowploughs were about to start for Magnolia. After all the summertime complaints from the village about potholes, and the city's absolute neglect of same, it seemed that the Mayor of Gloucester had raised the priority for Magnolia's streets. But the four crewmen, being civil servants, were sitting in the cabs of their vehicles, consulting maps, drinking coffee, and doing other things that civil servants are wont to do in almost every country.

'So what do we do now?' Molly asked impatiently.

'We wait,' laughed Tim. 'Turn on the radio.' She did, switching to the FM band, watching for the classical music of WVCA-FM.

'I'd do better with a little country music,' Tim suggested.

'Well, I wouldn't,' she protested. 'This is the only one-man radio station left in the United States. You surely remember Mr Geller, Tim?'

'Good lord, is he still operating?'

'As you hear,' she laughed. 'Owner, technician,

salesman, disc-jockey, he still does it all, right from his own living-room.'

'And the only time the station goes off the air is when he has to go out on an errand,' Tim recalled, watching the ploughs steadily. 'Well, that did the trick. Maybe they don't like Mozart? Here we go: Canticle for two snowploughs and a Bronco, in C Minor!'

'And the first thing we have to do when we get home,' Molly decided, 'is to find Moira's hearing aid.'

'No need to make a problem out of it,' Tim replied. 'She has two spares in her luggage, and a boxful of spare batteries.' Tapping Moira on the shoulder, Molly repeated the conversation by signs. The little girl giggled. 'I really don't need them,' she signed in return. 'You don't need batteries for signing, and my dad says we have to keep down the expenses.'

'Why did he say that?' Molly signed.

'Because he said weddings are expensive,' the child returned.

'Would you two cut that out,' Tim challenged. 'It isn't polite to whisper when other people are present.' As he spoke, Molly was translating into sign.

'Yes, sir,' his daughter said dutifully.

'Yes, sir indeed,' his future wife responded, but the two pairs of fingers kept up the conversation, and, after all, he had to keep his eyes on the road!

They followed the ploughs in lonely convoy until they reached the turn-off for Hesperus, and since that was the way the DPW was going, they followed right along. As a result they edged their way down to Norman Avenue, where two trucks from the electric company were doing their best to replace a pole, and out to Magnolia Avenue, where the ploughs made a great circle and turned back the way they had come. The great stormclouds had finally gathered up their skirts and departed. A three-quarter moon displayed a smile, and the myriad stars of winter sparkled like cold lights in the heavens.

Tim stopped the car at that point and went over to have a few words with the drivers. Watching through the cleared windshield, Molly smiled as she saw Tim's hand dive into a pocket and pass something to the older driver. As he sauntered back she could see he was whistling, and the plough was reversing its direction.

'They volunteered to plough all the way up to the house,' he grinned as he slid into the warmth of the truck. 'My lord, it's cold out there! They say that the storm wasn't so bad just to the south of us, and the routes through to Boston are all ploughed already. How's that for efficiency?'

'Only you could do it, Tim,' Molly teased him solemnly.

'How true!' That grin was back again, boyish, cheerful, memory-provoking, as he shifted into gear and followed the spume of snow from the plough.

CHAPTER TEN

THE plough made a great deal of noise as it roared almost to the edge of the bluff, where it turned around and clanked back towards the village centre. The old house was lit up from end to end, a signal that power had been restored in the neighbourhood. Gerda was waiting for them at the front door as the three walked through the crunchy dry snow.

'You were so late we didn't know when to expect you,' said Gerda. 'How's my baby?'

'Where's my Bertie?' Moira interrupted urgently, not realising the others were talking. 'I want my puppy!'

'Of course you do,' Aunt Gerda said gently. 'I moved the box into the hallway. Here he is, the tired little darling.'

Molly took over the sleeping puppy, displayed him to Moira, then explained to Gerda, 'She's fine, but she's lost her hearing aid. I'll take her up and get her settled, then——'

'I didn't know when to expect you, so I thought we'd go ahead with the meal,' Aunt Gerda explained. 'But we've only just sat down.'

'In which case, since you've done all the work so far, Tim, why don't you go in and start your meal? I'll take this little miss up and then come join you when she's comfortable.'

'I can take her up, Molly.' Tim had lost all his sophisticated appearance; it was a harried father speaking.

'So can I. And I want to.' Molly dropped a protective arm around Moira's shoulder, and the little girl snuggled up at her side. Tim, tired, perturbed, saw quickly that she was not to be stirred.

'Go ahead in,' he told Aunt Gerda. 'I'll wash up in the kitchen and join you.' Molly encouraged Moira to walk up the stairs, moving slowly. She could hear the clatter of dishes and conversation from the dining-room, and it gave her a little stab of pain. Poor pale Moira, tucked under her arm so closely, could hear nothing without her aid. She steered the little girl into her own bedroom, helped her undress, and tucked her into a long flannel nightgown before taking time to root out one of the spare hearing aids.

'I'm all right,' the child said, studying Molly's face in order to read her lips as she adjusted the volume of her replacement aid.

'I'm glad,' her adopted aunt said slowly, repeating in sign language. 'Tell me again about your puppy—your dog?'

'Bertie went missing,' Moira said in a rush. 'I didn't think he could jump out of that box, he must have. I hunted the whole house and couldn't find him. And then you said that about waking Shag, so I did. Your dog went to the front door and scratched, so I grabbed my coat and opened the door—and then he ran like blazes for the observation platform, and he jumped up at the edge of that stone garbage thing, so I looked inside, and there was Bertie, lying in the bottom, just squirming and crying. It was kind of hard to get him out 'cause that garbage thing is so deep, but I got my hands on him, only when I tried to stand up I slipped on the ice, and that's all I remember until you were there.'

'You didn't see anyone else?' Molly signed.

'No. Not nobody.'

'All right, love. Now, I'm going to get a washcloth and clean you up a little bit, and then I want you to take a good long nap.'

'But I'll miss Daddy's birthday party!' The child was so excited that she had to do the signs twice. Her vocabulary was extensive, but her fingers were not yet nimble enough.

'Not to worry,' Molly signed. 'Your daddy is a thousand years old, and I'll save you a piece of cake. Right?'

'Right.' Moira laughed for the first time since coming home, picked up Bertie from Molly's arms, and climbed into bed, where she became instantly solemn. 'I feel safer now with you here,' the child said, and lifted up both her arms in the signal for a hug. Molly leaned over and provided that service. 'I love you, Aunt Molly,' the child whispered in her ear. 'I've never been so happy, not any time or anywhere. Daddy tried to explain to me—about what was going to happen to me. He always said, "Be brave." And I wanted to be because *he* wanted it. But I was always scared. It frightened me. But now I've got you, and I think I can face it.' And then, much more wistfully, 'I wish—I wish I could just wave my magic wand and that *other* person would disappear!' Molly dabbed at her own eye to stop the little tear, and went for the washcloth. By the time she returned from the bathroom both Moira and little Bertie were fast asleep again.

So it was back to the bathroom for a very thoughtful Molly, where she managed to put her own face and person back in order while she gave the whole evening a good think. Sorting for the truth was like trying to follow a straight line through a well-planted maze. There was little Moira and her happiness, Tim and his confusion, Susan and her hatred, and even Gerda with her—scheming?

Only Captain Francis stood unaccused—well, that of which he *might* be accused was a simple problem between two consenting adults, as the new state laws described it. Molly shrugged that off.

But Tim—there was *another* problem entirely. He claimed that he wanted to marry her. But his reasons were so mixed that Molly could hardly decide what to do. Did he want to marry her for Moira's sake? That stood high on the list—very high. Or was his offer merely a ploy to get Susan out of his hair. That too rated highly. Certainly unrated was the crazy idea that he had finally fallen in love with Molly Patterson. Nice going, girl, she told her mirror image. You win first price for wild imagination! And with that she shrugged, tugged her blouse around in front, and marched herself down the corridor. In Susan's room she busied herself for a few minutes, then headed for the stairs. It was not sweet soft-hearted Molly going down those stairs, though. She *had* come to *some* answers; it was Joan of Arc Patterson stepping very determinedly down the old staircase, with more than a little anger in her eyes. And perhaps, she thought, with the strength of a fairy godmother, to do a little wand-waving?

They were all at table, having arrived at the main course, the Cornish rock hen, and conversation was fulsome. Molly peered into the dining-room. Captain Francis was sitting nearest to the door. At her small noise he looked around, and she beckoned. He excused himself from the table and joined her in the hall, where she murmured some very firm directions, at which he smiled, agreed, and escorted her back to the table.

'All's well?' Tim asked anxiously.

'All's well with Moira,' Molly qualified her answer. The table talk was renewed. Tim was at the far side of the big round table, with Gerda on his left and Susan on his right. Captain Francis had the chair beside Gerda, and Molly took the place opposite Tim. It irritated her intolerably. She managed two bites in a matter of twenty minutes. When the others had completely demolished their servings, hers was still big enough to feed a grown man. Shag, who grew fat on the leavings of others, sensed this and moved close to her leg. She patted the old dog's head. Ordinarily he knew better than to beg openly, but for this once, this night, Molly needed all the sympathy and support she could gather. And still her anger grew. Sweet, lovable Molly Patterson was out for blood!

'Well, I'll bring in the cake, shall I?' said Gerda. 'A special—Tim asked for it, I made the cake, and Molly decorated it.' The men made half-hearted moves to get up as she rose and went to the kitchen. In a moment she was back, bearing the massive cake. The strawberry juice was running freely; the whipped cream was a little liquid too. The whole thing looked like a mushy red and white confection.

'Just the way I like it,' said Tim with a big grin. 'But then Molly knows everything about me, so one would expect the perfect cake!'

A lot you know, buster, Molly told herself as she rose in her place. What I know about you—for sure—could be written on the back of one of the new twenty-five-cent postage stamps with a heavy-duty pen! But this is all the time I intend to wait!

'I have a small problem to be solved before you cut the cake,' she announced. The conversation stopped. Tim frowned, Susan glared, and the other couple looked as if they were holding hands under the tablecloth—and holding their breaths as well.

'Go ahead,' Tim invited cautiously.

Molly pushed her chair back and walked around so that she was standing between Tim and Susan. 'A long time ago,' she said quietly, 'a very dishonest woman stole my man.' Susan was laughing up at her; Tim's mouth was half open. 'But I deserved that, so it didn't set me off. And then that same woman was monstrously cruel to a very lovable child who couldn't defend herself.' Susan had lost her smile; Tim shifted anxiously in his seat, as if a flock of soldier ants were invading the chair. Gerda and her Captain leaned back in their chairs, very self-satisfied.

'But I can't act on something like that, because she wasn't my child—at that time.' Molly folded her arms over her breasts and took a deep breath.

'But then this same woman did a very terrible thing to a little dog—and that's where I draw the line!' Her voice had been gradually rising up-scale, until at the end of the sentence she was in full voice. Susan was turning various shades of pink, her mouth working at a rebuttal.

'You can't prove that,' she snarled, half rising. Molly put one hand on top of Susan's head and pushed her back down into the seat.

'I can't?' she retorted. 'And me an old Perry Mason fan? Well, let's see. Whoever was responsible took that puppy by the scruff of his neck, carried him outside in below-freezing weather, and dumped him into the old stone garbage container—and left him there to die!'

Susan made one more effort to get up. 'Prove it,' she snarled again, baring her lovely teeth like a mastiff.

'Yes, prove it,' Molly sighed. 'But first, while Moira was hunting that puppy, with Shag's help, she slipped on the ice and almost did herself a serious damage.'

'Do you think I'd do something like that to hurt my own daughter?' Susan screamed.

'Yes, I do,' Molly returned calmly.

'Then prove it!'

'Yes, prove it,' murmured Molly. 'Did you know that if you wet a dog's fur with some smelly liquid the dog will smell for hours and hours?'

Susan looked down at her hands, squirrelled up out of her chair, and backed away from Molly, holding her hands behind her back.

'Did you know that today, in this house, I rubbed Tim's back with eucalyptus oil?'

'So then you're the one who handled the dog!' Susan screamed. She was shaking, and almost seemed to be frothing at the mouth.

'Not exactly,' Molly continued inexorably. 'When I gave Tim that massage I wore rubber gloves. Tim got all his share on his back, so it couldn't have been him. But you, Susan. Remember? You spilled the bottle of oil, and it ran all over your hands? Remember, Susan?' Molly took a step in her cousin's direction, and Susan raised her hands defensively. 'And when you picked up the puppy, Susan, remember—you spread that eucalyptus oil all over Bertie's fur. Remember?'

'Tim, I don't know what this madwoman is talking about! Tim?'

'I'm very interested to hear,' he said judiciously, not moving a muscle.

'And let me tell you,' Molly continued, spitting the words out one at a time like slugs from a submachine gun, 'there's nothing in this world I hate worse than a person who would abuse a little dog just for the sake of vengeance.'

'You're mad,' Susan stammered. 'Totally mad!'

'Probably,' Molly continued. 'But this is *my* house, and I don't intend that you contaminate it for another second, Susan, cousin or no.' With which she leaned over Susan's place at the table, picked up her glass of red wine, and gently poured it all over the other woman's head.

'Well, you can't put me out on a night like this,' Susan spluttered. 'Tim, you can't let her——'

'It's Molly's house,' Tim said nonchalantly as he tossed her a napkin. 'I can't stop her if she wants to throw you out. In fact, I might even cheer a little.'

'Why, you——' Susan seized one of the silver candlesticks on the table and tried to used it as a club. One step forward, Molly told herself, and then turn, and—once again, just the way it had been explained in her martial arts class, there she was with the candlestick on the floor, and Susan's hand locked up behind her back in a painful hammer-lock. And with that hold in place, Molly urged her cousin towards the door, where Captain Francis was already waiting, the suitcase that Molly had just packed in his hand.

Molly halted the procession at the door, and turned. 'You will all excuse me?' she asked politely.

Ten minutes later she was standing in the cold doorway, rubbing her hands in a washing gesture as her Bronco, with Captain Francis at the wheel and a suddenly subdued Susan at his side, ploughed down the street and turned westward towards the Boston highway. When the red lights on the back of the truck faded out of sight, Molly shut the door gently and went back into the dining-room, shivering from anger more than from the cold. The others had hardly moved in her absence.

When she reappeared, both Gerda and Tim gave her a smile of welcome, although Tim's seemed just the tiniest bit apprehensive. She plumped into her seat at the foot of the table. 'I guess we're ready for the candles and cake now,' she said softly. In that one short period of time she had run out all her anger—well, almost all. And here was

Gerda, with those concerned eyes, and Tim, with those——

'She's gone?' he asked.

'Yes. The Captain is taking her to Logan Airport. And I don't think she'll ever come back. Not after our last few words.'

'I never would have expected it of sweet lovable Molly,' Tim chuckled. 'It did my heart good!' He jumped at that second, as if his aunt might have kicked his ankle under the table.

'It was a surprise,' Gerda said. 'But then I always knew you had it in you, Molly Patterson. Now, if we can put all that nastiness behind us, where the devil is that lawyer fellow?'

'Alfred?' Molly mused. 'Well, I—made him a proposition at the hospital, and he decided—he decided he didn't want to play in my league after all. I can see Alfred now, trying to borrow enough money to get back to the big city.'

'Well, then' said Tim in a burst of false enthusiasm, 'maybe we could drink a toast?'

'To what?' Molly, suspicious even of her lifelong love, felt that something was missing.

'To what?' Tim grinned. 'Why, how about this? You've solved all my problems, Molly Patterson, and now you won't *have* to marry me if you don't want to!'

A deadly silence came over the room. Molly staggered to her feet and stared over the distance between them. Too far. She pushed her chair away and this time walked round to stand between Gerda and Tim. He sat still, almost frozen in position.

'You're telling me, Tim Holland, that you don't want to marry me? That your proposal was all a trick?' Ice words from an ice maiden!

'No,' he responded anxiously. 'I'm not telling you that at all. I'm telling you that if you don't want to marry me, you don't have to.'

'You know something,' she mused, 'I've loved you for a long time, Timmy. But in between spates of loving, I think I've hated you. Did you know that?' Her desperately searching eyes travelled the table, and found what she wanted.

'Now, Molly,' he protested. 'Molly, you don't want to do that!'

'Don't I?' she shouted at him as she picked up the juicy mess that was his birthday cake. 'Don't I really, Tim Holland? Well, you unconscionable—oaf—I think I've wanted to do this since I was eight years old!' And with that she cradled the cake in both hands, and very gently pushed the entire mess into his face.

Tim sat there quietly, with strawberries and whipped cream gradually oozing downward across the bridge of his patrician nose. Gerda was quietly applauding. Molly, shocked back to sensibility, was appalled at what she had done. She backed away from them both a step at a time, until her nerve broke. The tears began, accompanied by the repressed sobs of a dozen years or more. She wheeled and ran for the front door.

Gerda was having trouble suppressing the laughter. When it finally broke loose she rolled in her chair, while her favourite nephew lifted one hand and cleared a strawberry out of his eye. 'There's hope for you yet, lad,' Aunt Gerda managed to choke out.

Tim shrugged his shoulders and his finger went to his mouth. 'Not as perfect as I thought,' he said philosophically. 'She didn't put enough sugar in the whipped cream.'

CHAPTER ELEVEN

MOLLY came back in out of the cold at eleven o'clock, about the time when Captain Francis arrived back from his trip to the airport. They entered hand in hand, the old man and the troubled young woman. Tim and Gerda had just finished the dishes, and were heading into the living-room to relax. Gerda came over and kissed the Captain on his cheek before offering him a brandy.

'Here's to crime,' he toasted. Tim smiled half-heartedly—cleaned-up Tim, with no trace of the shortcake in view. Gerda joined the toast. Molly, who had decided in the last twenty minutes to give up alcohol and men and to enter a nunnery—if any still existed—flopped herself down in a chair.

'So where did you leave the spider lady?' Gerda asked.

'At the airport,' the Captain responded. 'She wasted the entire trip mouthing off about how bad New England was, and how she hated it, and the snow, and the people. But mostly about the snow.'

'You just dropped her off at the terminal?'

'Oh, no,' he laughed. 'Miss Molly here asked me to give her any help that I could, so I did. She wanted a ticket on the first plane out of the city, she told me.' He stopped long enough to take a sip from the brandy glass. There was a laugh hiding under his bushy grey eyebrows.

'So don't sit on it,' Gerda commanded. 'Where was the flight going?'

'Well, there wasn't any choice,' the Captain mused. 'The airport had just reopened. She didn't ask me any

185

questions, just got on the plane at the gate. It was a charter flight, headed for Nome, Alaska.'

'Yes, that will be great,' said Gerda in awe. 'You old reprobate! Luckily they don't have snow in Nome at this time of year.'

'Yeah,' the Captain responded. 'Let's you and me go in the kitchen and talk. This fancy living-room leaves me nervous.'

'Yeah, talk,' said Aunt Gerda, and winked at Tim as she followed Captain Francis out of the room.

'That pair,' Tim said after a moment of silence. 'They've debated it for thirty years or more, but she tells me they've decided to get married.'

'Lucky,' Molly sighed. 'Tim——'

'Molly——' he said at exactly the same time. They both laughed nervously. 'You first,' he said. 'Ladies first.'

'I'm not a lady,' she told him, disgusted with herself. 'And I'm not about to apologise for dumping that cake all over you. I'm not sorry—I enjoyed that very much. It's been something I've wanted to do for years.'

'Yes, I could tell,' he replied solemnly. 'Even an oaf like me gets the message after while.'

'Tim——' she stammered. '*That* part—I do apologise for that. You're not an oaf. Well, not very often, anyway, but——'

'I think you'd better let me have my say first,' he interrupted as he came over and sat down beside her. 'We have to go back ten years, to your eighteenth birthday, Molly. Remember?'

'I could never forget,' she sighed.

'Nor me either, Molly.' She had been staring straight ahead up until that moment. Now she turned and looked squarely at him. 'Do you know why I came over that morning?'

'I—didn't remember your coming in the morning,' she half-whispered. He was leading her back into the dark jungle-land of horrors, of things she didn't want to remember.

'I thought your father was going to tell you,' he sighed. 'I came over to ask you to marry me.'

'But—Tim? I don't understand. You didn't ask—and you married Susan!'

'I know. Look, Moll. Your father invited me into the den. He said he had something important to say. I followed him. Susan was there, waiting for us. And your father told me that Susan was pregnant—and I was the man! I know that Moira's age has puzzled you ever since we came back, my dear. Susan and I were married ten years ago; Moira is nine and a half years old.'

'Oh, God, Tim. Then it was true?' Molly buried her face in her hands and sniffed back the tears.

'It *could* have been true,' he muttered. 'It wasn't, but it *could* have been. That's why I went along with it. Susan and I tried it on one time. It wasn't until a couple of years later that I found out that every dog on the north shore had been sniffing around Susan. She should have sold tickets to keep the men in order. When she discovered she was pregnant she picked me out of the crowd because my family had the money. That's not much of an excuse, Moll, but I was a hot-blooded kid, and she was offering without strings—and I really screwed up our lives, Molly, yours and mine.'

'But, Tim, you never said a word to me. And you were gone—ever so long!'

'I had no right to say anything to you, Molly. I'd done the deed, and I figured it was up to me to make the marriage work. But instead—well, you know what happened now. And what could I do after my divorce? I didn't have the nerve to come back here looking for you—I thought at first that you would have been snapped up by one of half a dozen men. And when Aunt Gerda told me that you were still single—I just couldn't understand.'

'But even then you didn't come back,' she accused as she lifted her head back up. Poor Tim, she thought, all those troubles. And I thought *I* had a hard time!

'No,' he sighed, 'I didn't come back. There was always Moira. Lord, Molly, I can't tell you—I wandered all over Europe, from one hospital to another, from one specialist to another. I didn't dare stop. There was always the thought that the next man was the one who could come up with the miraculous cure! So I stayed away—until the last man, at Heidelberg, told me that the chase was fruitless.'

'And here you are,' she concluded.

'And here we are,' he agreed sombrely.

Molly sat quietly, thinking. Tim moved a little closer. Out of the corner of her eye she could see his hands signalling, but her mind paid no attention. Dear Tim, and Moira too. I *want* that dear little scrap to be my own. I *want* her. But do you marry a man because you want his daughter to be yours? That makes for a strange sort of marriage, doesn't it? Can I marry for Moira's sake? Or would I do better to skip the wedding and just be a maiden aunt? Look at Gerda. All the years she's spent, avoiding the fact that she loved the Captain. Can you see Molly Patterson, forty years from now, doddering up to Tim Holland and saying, 'Tim, we should have gotten married all those years ago!'

Suddenly something pierced her cloud of thought. Her head snapped around and she stared at the tall thin lovable man sitting next to her. His hands were signing something, over and over again. 'I love you.'

'Tim,' she said tentatively. 'We were fooling you, Moira and I. That doesn't mean *good morning*.'

'I know what it means,' he answered gruffly. 'Aunt Gerda gave me a book of American Sign on Thanksgiving morning. I just didn't have the nerve to say it out loud!'

'Oh, Tim!' All her speculations collapsed, all her battle flags surrendered. With a little cry of happiness Molly hurled herself at the man who had once left her behind. Like a puppy she coiled up in his lap and squirmed to get as close to him as possible. His warm kiss was the seal. She gave herself up.

Out in the kitchen the two schemers listened intently. 'Well,' Aunt Gerda whispered, 'either they've made up, or he's killed her.'

'Or she's killed him,' the Captain corrected. 'But I have the feeling that your witchery has succeeded. Not only in there; out here too. This sitting around on hard chairs is not for people our age, love, no matter what those two are up to. What do you say—shall we go upstairs?'

Coming soon
to an easy chair near you.

FIRST CLASS is Harlequin's armchair travel plan for the incurably romantic. You'll visit a different dreamy destination every month from January through December without ever packing a bag. No jet lag, no expensive air fares and *no* lost luggage. Just First Class Harlequin Romance reading, featuring exotic settings from Tasmania to Thailand, from Egypt to Australia, and more.

FIRST CLASS romantic excursions guaranteed! Start your world tour in January. Look for the special **FIRST CLASS** destination on selected Harlequin Romance titles—there's a new one every month.

NEXT DESTINATION:
GREECE

 Harlequin Books

JTR4

COMING IN 1991 FROM
HARLEQUIN SUPERROMANCE:

Three abandoned orphans,
one missing heiress!

Dying millionaire Owen Byrnside receives an
anonymous letter informing him that twenty-six years
ago, his son, Christopher, fathered a daughter. The
infant was abandoned at a foundling home that
subsequently burned to the ground, destroying all
records. Three young women could be Owen's long-
lost granddaughter, and Owen is determined to track
down each of them! Read their stories in

#434 HIGH STAKES (available January 1991)
#438 DARK WATERS (available February 1991)
#442 BRIGHT SECRETS (available March 1991)

Three exciting stories of intrigue and romance by
veteran Superromance author Jane Silverwood.

Harlequin Intrigue®

A SPAULDING & DARIEN MYSTERY
by Robin Francis

An engaging pair of amateur sleuths—Jenny Spaulding and Peter Darien—were introduced to Harlequin Intrigue readers in #147, BUTTON, BUTTON (Oct. 1990). Jenny and Peter will return for further spine-chilling romantic adventures in April 1991 in #159, DOUBLE DARE in which they solve their next puzzling mystery. Two other books featuring Jenny and Peter will follow in the A SPAULDING AND DARIEN MYSTERY series.

IBB-1A

HARLEQUIN
Romance®

Coming Next Month

#3115 ARROGANT INVADER Jenny Arden
There had never been much love lost between Gwenyth Morgan and
Jeb Hunter, though now he seems determined to pursue her. But since
Gwenyth is happily engaged to Marc and planning a future in France, what is
there to be afraid of?

#3116 LOVE'S AWAKENING Rachel Ford
Just sixteen when she'd been emotionally blackmailed into marrying
Alex Petrides, Selina had run away within hours of the wedding. Alex hadn't
followed as she'd expected. Now, three years later, something irresistibly
draws her back to Greece.

#3117 THE ONLY MAN Rosemary Hammond
Her father's death and her fiancé's jilting leaves Jennie in shock. Then
Alex Knight, her father's friend, gives her a home and a job at his winery. But
Alex treats her as a child when Jennie longs to be recognized as a woman....

#3118 TWO AGAINST LOVE Ellen James
Christie Daniels has just managed to escape one domineering man—her
father—when she's confronted with another. Matt Gallagher's mission is to
talk her into leaving her New Mexico bed-and-breakfast and returning to her
father's brokerage firm in New York City. Christie has no intention of
agreeing, but she *does* wish Matt weren't so darned attractive....

#3119 AN UNCOMMON AFFAIR Leigh Michaels
Marsh Endicott mistakenly thinks Torey Farrell will be pleased to sell him her
half share of the house they jointly inherited. Torey, though, can't wait to
start a new life in the house—and certainly doesn't want a ready-made,
already engaged housemate!

#3120 RITES OF LOVE Rebecca Winters
Courtney Blake, who's half Miccosukee, accuses the man she loves of
betraying the tribe's faith in him. She flees to her mother's family in the
Everglades, but Jonas follows her—and forces her to confront her own lack of
faith in their love.

Available in April wherever paperback books are sold, or through
Harlequin Reader Service:

In the U.S.
P.O. Box 1397
Buffalo, N.Y.
14240-1397

In Canada
P.O. Box 603
Fort Erie, Ontario
L2A 5X3